TRAIN ROBBERY

Boyd heard a shot fired from inside the baggage car. That was followed almost immediately by more shots from outside the car, the gun blasts lighting up the darkness with their muzzle flashes.

"Throw out the money pouch, or we'll kill you!" one of the robbers shouted.

Boyd saw the money pouch tossed from the train. He aimed at the robber who was waiting for it, then squeezed off a shot just as it hit the robber's hands.

The bullet plowed into the robber's chest. The robber was knocked from his horse and he lay flat on his back on the ground with both arms spread out to either side. The money pouch lay beside him.

"Deermont!" a voice shouted from the darkness. "Get the money!"

One of the other riders leaned to pick up the money pouch. Boyd fired a second round . . .

M^cMASTERS

PLUNDER VALLEY

Lee Morgan

J

JOVE BOOKS, NEW YORK

PLUNDER VALLEY

A Jove Book / published by arrangement with
the author

PRINTING HISTORY
Jove edition / October 1995

ISBN: 0-515-11731-5

A JOVE BOOK®
Jove Books are published by The Berkley Publishing Group,
200 Madison Avenue, New York, New York 10016.
JOVE and the "J" design are trademarks
belonging to Jove Publications, Inc.

PRINTED IN THE UNITED STATES OF AMERICA

10   9   8   7   6   5   4   3   2   1

PLUNDER VALLEY

One

The Mogollon Mountains, New Mexico Territory

Curly Dobbs lay on top of a flat rock, looking back along the trail over which they had just come. He saw the single rider unerringly following them.

"Is he still there?" Frank asked.

"Yeah," Curly growled. "I believe that son of a bitch could track a fish through water."

Frank and Curly Dobbs and their cousins, Matt and Luke Anderson, were on the run. A week earlier they had raided the Rocking P Ranch just outside of the ranching community of Kettle Springs. They waited outside the house until sunup, then they broke in on rancher Nate Pemberton and his family at breakfast. They killed Pemberton and his sixteen-year-old son, Edward, then they raped and killed Pemberton's wife, Ella, and their fifteen-year-old daughter, Sue, each man taking turns with each one of them. After that they helped themselves to the breakfast Ella Pemberton had prepared, then they stole fifty head of prime beef and moved them up to the railhead at Demming where the cattle were sold at thirty dollars a head for shipment back East.

"Who'd you say that fella was that's trailin' us?" Matt asked.

"I heard his name spoke back in Demming," Frank said. "Somebody said his name was McMasters. Boyd McMasters."

Matt snorted. "Never heard of him."

"Me neither," Curly said. He pointed back down the trail. "But I'll say this for the son of a bitch. Once he gets his teeth into you, he don't give up. We've tried ever' trick in the book to shake him off our tail, and he's still there."

What the Dobbs and Anderson brothers did not realize was that the family they had massacred came under the protection of the Cattleman's Protective Association. Nate Pemberton had been a member in good standing of the New Mexico Cattleman's Association. When that organization's officers, up in Sante Fe, learned what had happened to one of their own, they asked the Cattleman's Protective Association for help. In response to their request, Boyd McMasters was sent to New Mexico to look into the case.

Boyd was a Captain in the Cattleman's Protective Association, which was the police arm of the Cattleman's Association. The Cattleman's Association enjoyed a large and influential membership from the states and territories of Texas, Indian Territories, Arkansas, New Mexico, Arizona, Nevada, Oregon, Colorado, Kansas, the Dakotas, Wyoming, Montana, Missouri, Nebraska and Iowa. Boyd's position in the Cattleman's Protective Association made him a de facto law enforcement officer who enjoyed a degree of authority that was accredited by the federal, state, county, and municipal agencies of those same states and territories. This gave him the jurisdiction to pursue wanted men across state and territory lines.

"What are we goin' to do about that son of a bitch? We can't shake him off," Frank growled.

Matt looked back toward the rider. "All right, let's go up through that draw," he said, pointing.

"That's a dead-end canyon," Luke replied. "Don't you 'member that, Matt? We was up here last year."

"I know it's a dead-end canyon," Matt said. "But it's got two or three good places in there where we can hide. All we got to do is let him follow us in there, then ambush him."

"What if he don't come in? What if he just stays back at the mouth of the canyon and waits us out?" Curly asked.

"Hell, there's only one of him. There's four of us," Matt insisted. "If he don't come in, we'll just come out and get him."

"Matt's right," Frank said. "Let's just kill this McMasters fella and get it over with."

"Come on, I know a perfect spot," Matt said.

Boyd McMasters had never been here before, but he had been in dozens of places just like this. And if he had to make a guess, he would say that this was a dead-end canyon. He stopped at the mouth of the canyon and took a drink from his canteen while he studied it. According to the information sent him by the Association, the Andersons lived in the New Mexico Territory and would know whether or not this was a dead-end canyon.

Maybe it wasn't dead-end. Maybe there was a way

out. Or, maybe they knew that it was dead-end, and wanted to go into it anyway. Why would they want to do that? he asked himself. Then he answered his own question: They figured they would be able to draw him in, then set up an ambush for him.

Boyd pulled his long gun out of the saddle holster, then he started walking into the canyon, leading his horse. The horse's hooves fell sharply on the stone floor and echoed loudly back from the canyon walls. The canyon made a forty-five degree turn to the left just in front of him, so he stopped. Right before he got to the turn he slapped his horse on the rump and sent it on through.

The canyon exploded with the sound of gunfire as the Dobbs and Andersons opened up on what they thought would be their pursuer. Instead, their bullets whizzed harmlessly over the empty saddle of the riderless horse, raised sparks as they hit the rocky ground, then whined off into empty space, echoing and re-echoing in a cacophony of whines and shrieks.

From his position just around the corner from the turn, Boyd located two of his ambushers. They were about a third of the way up the north wall of the canyon, squeezed in between the wall itself and a rock outcropping that provided them with a natural cover. Or so they thought.

The firing stopped and, after a few seconds of dying echoes, the canyon grew silent.

"Where the hell is he?" one of the ambushers yelled, and Boyd could hear the last two words repeated in echo down through the canyon. *". . . is he, is he, is he?"*

Boyd studied the rock face of the wall just behind the spot where he had located two of them, then he began firing. His rifle boomed loudly, the thunder of the detonating cartridges picking up resonance through the canyon and doubling then re-doubling in intensity. Boyd wasn't even trying to aim at the two men, but was, instead, taking advantage of the position in which they had placed themselves. He fired several rounds, knowing that the bullets were splattering against the rock wall behind the two men, fragmenting into deadly, whizzing flying missiles of death. He emptied his rifle. Then, as the echoes thundered back through the canyon, he began reloading.

"Curly!" a strained voice called. "Curly!"

"What is it?" another voice answered. This voice was from the other side of the narrow draw, halfway up on the opposite wall.

"Curly, we're both killed."

"What?"

There was no answer.

"Matt!"

Silence.

"Luke!"

More silence.

"Matt, Luke, are you all right?"

There was no answer.

Boyd changed positions, then searched the opposite canyon wall. There was silence for a long time, then, as he knew they would, his quarry began to get anxious. He saw first one then the other pop up to have a look around.

"Curly, Frank," Boyd shouted. And the echo repeated the names. *"Curly, Frank. Curly, Frank. Curly, Frank."*

"What do you want? . . . *want, want, want?"*

"I want you to throw your guns down and give yourselves up," Boyd said.

"Why should we do that?"

For his answer, Boyd raised his rifle and shot at the wall just behind Curly and Frank, creating the same effect he had with Matt and Luke. The only difference was that he shot only one round, and he placed it to give a demonstration of what he could do . . . not to kill.

"Son of a bitch!" one of the two men shouted.

"I can take you out of there just the way I did the Andersons," Boyd said. "Or I can let you wait up there until you run out of water. You didn't take your canteens with you, did you?"

Boyd was running a bluff. He couldn't see well enough to determine whether they had their canteens or not. He would bet, however, that if they thought they would be able to ambush him and kill him quickly, then they didn't think to take their canteens with them. It was actually a double bluff, because when Boyd sent his own horse through, he had not removed his canteen either.

There was no response from the Dobbses, so Boyd waited a few minutes, then he fired a second time. The boom sounded like a cannon blast, and he heard the scream of the bullet, followed once more by a curse.

"By now you've probably figured out that I can make one bullet do the work of about ten," Boyd said. "If I shoot again, I'm going to put them where they can do the most damage . . . same as I did with the Andersons. You've got five seconds to give yourselves up, or die."

Boyd raised his rifle.

"No, wait! . . . *wait, wait, wait!*" the terrified word echoed through the canyon. "We're comin' down! . . . *down, down, down!*"

"Throw your weapons down first."

Boyd saw hands appear, then pistols and rifles started tumbling down the side of the canyon, rattling and clattering until they reached the canyon floor.

"Put your hands up, then step out where I can see you," Boyd ordered.

The two men, moving hesitantly, edged out from behind the rocky slab where they had taken cover. They held their hands over their heads.

"Come on down here," Boyd invited.

Stepping gingerly, the two climbed down the wall until, a moment later, they were standing in front of Boyd. Boyd handcuffed each of them.

"What are you goin' to do with us?" Curly asked.

"I'm going to take you back to Kettle Springs to stand trial," Boyd explained.

"How we goin' to ride like this? We can't stay in the saddle with our hands handcuffed behind us like this. We'll fall off."

Boyd smiled at them. "Well, stay on as long as you can, boys," he said. "And when you fall off, I'll help you on again."

Red Dog Saloon, Kettle Springs, Six Weeks Later

"Oyez, oyez, oyez, this here court is about to reconvene, the honorable Judge Amon T. Boggs presiding," the bailiff shouted. "Everybody stand respectful. Lennie, you make dead certain you don't serve no liquor durin' the hearin' of the verdict and the sentencin' to be hung."

"The bar is still closed, Tom. I ain't served a drop since the trial started."

The honorable Amon T. Boggs came out of the back

room of the saloon and took a seat at his "bench," which was merely the best table in the saloon. The table sat upon a raised platform, which had been built just for this purpose. Court was being held in the Red Dog Saloon because it was the largest and most substantial building in Kettle Springs. The saloon was also the easiest place to empanel a jury, for it was always crowded, making it easy for the judge to round up twelve sober men, good and true. If it was sometimes difficult to find twelve sober men then the judge could stretch the definition of sobriety thin enough to meet the needs of the court. The "good and true," however, had to be taken upon faith.

The trial of Charles "Curly" Dobbs and Frank Dobbs took no more than an hour. The jury's deliberation lasted only five minutes. Then the jury sent word that they had reached a verdict, thus causing the court to be reconvened.

After taking his seat at the "bench," Judge Amon Boggs adjusted the glasses on the end of his nose then cleared his throat.

"Would the bailiff please bring the prisoners before the bench?"

The bailiff, who was leaning against the bar with his arms folded across his chest, spit a quid of tobacco into the brass spittoon, then leaned over the Dobbs brothers.

"Get up, you two," he growled. "Present yourself before the judge."

The Dobbs brothers were handcuffed together, and they had shackles on their ankles. They shuffled up to stand in front of the judge.

"Mr. Foreman of the jury, have you reached a verdict?" the judge asked.

"We have, Your Honor."

"What is the verdict?"

"Your Honor, we have found these guilty sons of bitches guilty," the foreman said.

"You goddamn well better have!" someone shouted from the court.

The judge banged his gavel on the table.

"Order!" he called. "I will have order in my court." He looked over at the foreman. "So say you all?" he asked.

"So say we all," the foreman replied.

The judge took off his glasses and began polishing them as he studied the two prisoners before him.

"Charles Dobbs and Frank Dobbs, you have been tried by a jury of your peers and you have been found guilty of the crimes of murder, rape, and robbery," he said. "Before this court passes sentence, have you anything to say?"

"Yeah," Curly snarled. "Pemberton's wife was one good fuck."

"And the fifteen year old girl was better," Frank put in.

The court gasped, then several men shouted out in anger.

"Hang the bastards! Hang 'en right here!"

Judge Boggs pounded his gavel again until, finally, order was restored. He glared at the two men for a long moment, then he cleared his throat.

"Charles Dobbs and Frank Dobbs, it is the sentence of this court that you be taken from this place and put in jail long enough to witness one more night pass from this mortal coil. At dawn's light on the morrow, you are to be taken from jail and transported to a place where you will be hanged.''

''Your Honor, we can't hang 'em in the mornin'. We ain't built no gallows yet,'' the sheriff said.

Judge Boggs held up his hand to silence the sheriff, indicating that he had already taken that into consideration. ''This court authorizes the use of a tree, a lamp post, a hay-loading stanchion, or any other device, fixture, apparatus, contrivance, agent, or means as may be sufficient to suspend your carcasses above the ground, bringing about the effect of breaking your neck, collapsing your windpipe, and, in any and all ways, squeezing the last breath of life from your worthless, vile, and miserable bodies.''

Twelve hours later

Deputy Simmons had been napping at his desk in the sheriff's office, when something . . . a noise, a change, maybe even a dream, awakened him.

''What?'' he asked, startled awake. ''What is it?'' He opened his eyes and looked around the inside of the sheriff's office. The room was dimly lit by a low-burning kerosene lantern. A plethora of Wanted posters fluttered from the bulletin board. A pot of aromatic coffee sat on a small, wood-burning stove. The Regulator clock on the wall swept its pendulum back and forth in a measured *tick-tock*, the hands on the face pointing to ten minutes after two. Simmons rubbed his eyes, then stood up and stretched. He went to the stove to pour himself a cup of coffee, then he stepped over to the jail cell to look inside. Both Curly and Frank Dobbs were sitting on their bunks.

"What's the matter?" Simmons asked. He took a slurping drink of his coffee. "Can't you fellas sleep any?"

"No," Frank growled.

"Well, I wouldn't worry about it," Simmons said. He took another drink of coffee. "In just about four more hours or so, you won't have any trouble at all goin' to sleep. You'll be sleepin' forever!" He laughed at his joke, then took another swallow of his coffee.

"Ahhh," he said. "Coffee is one of the sweetest pleasures of life, don't you think? But then, life itself is sweet, ain't it?" He laughed again, then turned away from the cell.

He gasped in surprise at seeing a Mexican standing between himself and his desk. He had not heard the Mexican come in. The Mexican was wearing an oversized sombrero, and he had a dark moustache which curved down along each side of his mouth.

"What the hell are you doin' in here, Mex?" Simmons asked, gruffly. "You aren't supposed to be in here."

"I have come to work, *señor*," the Mexican said. He made a motion as if he were sweeping the floor. "Sweep floor."

"Sweep the floor at two o'clock in the morning? Are you crazy? Get the hell out of here!"

"Deputy?" Curly called.

"Now, what the hell do you want?" Simmons asked, turning back toward the jail cell. He was surprised to see both Curly and Frank grinning broadly.

"I want you to be nicer to our friend, Paco," Curly said, easily.

"To Paco?" Simmons asked, confused by the strange

remark. Suddenly he realized what he had done! He had just turned his back on the Mexican.

Too late, Simmons felt the Mexican's hand come around to clasp over his mouth. Simmons dropped his cup of coffee and started reaching for his gun. That was a mistake, for even as his fingers wrapped around the grip of his pistol, he felt something sharp at his throat. The Mexican's hand flashed quickly across his neck. There was a stinging sensation, then a wetness at his collar. The Mexican let go of him and stepped back. Simmons felt his legs turn to rubber, and he fell to the floor. He put his hand up to his neck, then pulled it away and looked in horror at the blood on his fingers. He tried to call out but could not because his windpipe had been cut and he could make no sound at all save the silent scream in his head.

As he was losing consciousness he saw the Mexican opening the cell door. The Dobbs brothers hurried out. Curly came over to look down at him.

"Deputy, when you get to hell, tell our cousins, Matt and Luke, hello for us, will you?" he asked.

"Horses in alley behind calaboose," Paco said. "Come."

"Not yet. We got a stop to make first," Curly said.

"Where?" Frank asked.

"The hotel."

"Why we goin' to the hotel?"

" 'Cause that's where the judge is," Curly explained.

Frank smiled. "Yeah," he said. "Yeah, that's a good idea."

The three men left the jail, then slipped through the dark shadows down the street to the Morning Star Hotel. They moved in through the front door, then walked quietly over to the counter. As the desk clerk snored loudly, they checked the registration book.

"He's in two-oh-three," Curly whispered.

Taking the spare key to the room, the three men left the desk clerk undisturbed, then moved quickly and quietly up to the second floor. They walked down the carpeted hallway until they found the door. Slowly, Curly unlocked the door, then pushed it open.

The judge was snoring loudly.

"The son of a bitch wasn't losin' no sleep over sentencin' us to hang, was he?" Curly whispered. He pulled his gun.

"*Non, señor,*" Paco said, shaking his head. He put his finger over his mouth, making a *shhh* sound.

"Paco's right," Frank whispered. "You use that gun, it's goin' to make too much noise."

"I kill him for you," Paco offered. Pulling his knife, Paco stepped over to the judge's bed.

"Wait!" Curly said. "I want the son of a bitch to wake up long enough to know what happened to him."

Paco nodded.

Curly put his hand on the judge's shoulder.

"Judge. Judge, wake up," he said.

The judge snorted, then opened his eyes.

"What is it? Who is there?"

"It's a couple of friends of yours, Judge. Curly and Frank Dobbs," Curly said. "We just killed the deputy and broke jail. Now we've come to kill you."

"What?" the judge gasped. He started to sit up but before he was halfway in the upright position, Paco's knife flashed, quickly, across his neck. The judge's eyes opened wide in shock and fear, and he put his hands up to his throat, then fell back down onto the pillow.

Curly stepped over to the window. "Let's go out this way," he suggested. "There's less chance anyone will see us. We can go up the alley to our horses."

Frank started looking around the room.

"Come on," Curly said. "What the hell are you lookin' for? You know this old fart doesn't have any money."

"This is what I was lookin' for," Frank said a moment later, holding something up which gleamed softly in the dim light.

"What is that?"

"The judge's gavel," Frank said, triumphantly. "I want something to remember this by."

Two

Sonora Desert, Arizona Territory

Boyd McMasters, carrying his saddle on one shoulder and his rifle on the other, trudged on through the long afternoon. Three miles behind him his horse lay dead, the victim of an unseen prairie-dog hole. Boyd had hated putting a bullet in the horse's brain, but as the horse had suffered a compound fracture of the right foreleg, he'd had no choice.

He didn't think he would have to walk too far, though. Earlier in the day he had seen smoke from a passing locomotive. That meant that not too far ahead of him there was a railroad.

Boyd was headed for the town of Crittenden. One of the services provided by the Cattleman's Protective Association was to appraise the strength and security of any bank that held a substantial amount of Association members' money. If the bank came up to the high standards set by the Association, then anyone who robbed or defrauded that bank would be subject to pursuit, arrest, and prosecution by the Association.

Six wealthy ranchers from the county had been keeping their money in a bank in Tucson, but they had recently transferred their accounts to the Territorial Bank of Crittenden. Boyd had drawn the assignment of validating the bank as deserving of the Association's protection.

He reached the railroad just as the sun was going down and he dropped his saddle and gear with a sigh of relief, then walked up the small grade to stand on the track. He squinted his brown eyes and scratched at the stubble of a sandy three-day growth of beard on an otherwise handsome face as he peered eastward down the track. Stretching northeast to southwest was a set of rails, shining gold now in the light of the setting sun. He dropped to his knees and placed an ear to one of the rails, then smiled, for he could hear the faint humming which told him that a train was approaching.

Boyd gathered enough firewood to build a signal fire, then he put it right in the middle of the track so the engineer would not miss it. When he had the wood laid, he drew his saddle and gear up close by the track and waited.

It was several moments more before the train appeared. Although it was approaching at about thirty miles an hour, the vastness of the terrain made it appear to be crawling. Against the distant purple of the Dragoon Mountains, the silhouette of the train seemed tiny, and from this distance even the smoke which poured from its diamond stack made little impression upon the vast panorama.

Boyd could hear the train quite clearly now. The puffing engine sound was Boyd's signal to light the fire and within a moment or two he had a blaze burning brightly.

He waited until he heard the sound of the engine brak-

ing before he picked up his saddle and gear. The train
ground to a reluctant halt, puffing black smoke and emit-
ting tendrils of white steam which shone red in the light
of the setting sun. Two faces appeared in the window
of the engine cab. One was clean shaven, and the other
sported a white beard. Boyd also saw the door of the
mail car slide open and a gun barrel protrude through
the narrow gap.

"What'd you stop us for?" the older man asked.

"I lost my horse," Boyd replied. "I need a ride into
Crittenden."

"Mister, we can't be pickin' up ever'one we pass.
Especially with what we're carryin'," the younger man
said.

"Billy Ray, don't go spoutin' off about what we're
carryin'," the engineer chastised.

"Sorry," Billy Ray said, contritely.

"I'm willin' to pay for my ride," Boyd offered.

The older man stroked his beard. "Billy Ray's right
about we shouldn't be stoppin'," he said. "And ordi-
narily I wouldn't have. But with all the rains we had
this week, I didn't know but what you might of been
signallin' me that the track was washed out ahead." He
sighed. "Okay, mister, climb aboard. You can pay the
conductor."

"Thanks," Boyd said. He started toward the rear of
the train, then climbed on at the first car behind the mail
car. He was met, immediately, by the conductor.

"Mister, what are you doin' here?" the conductor
asked.

"Your engineer picked me up."

"That was a damn fool thing for him to do."

"Under the circumstances, I thought it was a right friendly act," Boyd said.

"Yeah, well, you never can tell when you stop like that, but what there might not be a band of robbers waiting out in the dark," the conductor said.

"Especially if you're carrying a lot of money," Boyd added.

The conductor's eyes narrowed. "How'd you know about the money?"

Boyd chuckled. "Didn't, exactly. The fireman sort of tipped me to it."

"Yeah, well, we're carrying ten thousand dollars to the bank in Crittenden. We got a extra guard on, but I'll feel better when we get shed of the money." He sighed. "All right, you're on now, so you may as well stay on. How far are you goin'?"

"Crittenden."

"That'll be a dollar and a half."

"Wasn't plannin' on buyin' the train, mister. I just want to ride on it," Boyd said.

"It's a dollar and a half, nevertheless, same as if you'd got on back in Tombstone. That's the rule of the Southern Pacific."

Boyd took out the money.

"You can leave your saddle and tack here in the vestibule," the conductor invited.

"Thanks," Boyd said, setting his saddle down. He kept his rifle.

"That, too, if you want."

Boyd looked at his rifle. "No," he said. "I'll keep this with me."

The conductor looked at the rifle.

"Don't think I've ever seen a gun quite like that."

Boyd held out his rifle for the conductor's closer inspection. It was a lever-action weapon, with a 48-inch octagonal barrel. But it was the bore which was most impressive.

"Is that a shotgun?"

"Nope," Boyd said. "It's a .70-caliber rifle."

"A rifle? My God, where did you ever find one with a bore that large?"

"Didn't find it," Boyd answered easily. "I made it." Boyd smiled. "So you can see why I'd just as soon keep it with me."

The rifle was more than just large. It was, in the hands of a skilled marksman, a gun of exceptional accuracy. Using it, Boyd had "fetched his mark" at distances of up to half a mile. And the energy of a bullet that large and that heavy was enough to knock down an adobe wall. There had been a few who, upon observing the gun in action, called the weapon a "shoulder cannon," and Boyd didn't disagree with them.

The rifle wasn't the only thing Boyd had worked on. He had also modified his Colt .44 revolvers so that the cylinders held seven cartridges instead of six. That modification wasn't quite as noticeable, however, so that to the casual observer, the pistols on his belt were no different from any other six-shooter.

Boyd stepped through the door of the car and, as the train began getting under way again, walked to the far end where he selected an empty seat in the last row. He sat down, put the rifle between himself and the window, then pulled his long legs up so that his knees were resting on the seat back in front of him. After that he reached up and casually tipped his hat forward, then folded his arms across his chest. Within moments, he was sound asleep.

It was dark, though the brightly shining moon provided a surprising amount of illumination. Jason Cantrell was sitting on a rock eating cold beans from a can. Cantrell was a man of medium height and size, distinguished only by his pockmarked face and a drooping left eye. The droop was the result of an old wound, suffered in a knife fight Cantrell had the first time he was ever in jail. The other prisoner had cut the muscles over the eyelid, leaving Cantrell permanently disfigured. Cantrell had cut the other man's jugular vein, leaving him permanently dead.

Porterfield had climbed up onto the ledge a little earlier and was looking toward the east. Michaels and Slater were down by the track and Deermont was relieving himself, no more than six feet away.

"Goddamnit, Deermont, you got no more manners than to piss that close to where a man is eatin'?" Cantrell growled.

"Sorry," Deermont said. "Wasn't thinkin'."

"That don't surprise me none. You don't never think."

"Hey, Cantrell, I can see the light," Porterfield called down. "The train's a'comin'."

Cantrell took the last mouthful of beans, wiped the spoon clean on his shirt, then stuck it in his pocket. He tossed the can over his shoulder and it landed with a soft clanking sound. He stood up and brushed his hands together.

"Michaels, Slater, get over here," Cantrell called.

Michaels and Slater came over to join Cantrell and the other two.

"Now, you got it straight what we're goin' to do?"

"Yeah," Michaels said. "We're goin' to build a fire to stop the train. Then when it stops, we'll keep the engineer and the fireman covered. Deermont is goin' to watch for the conductor or anyone else on the train, while Porterfield puts a stick of dynamite on the door of the mail car. When it goes, me and Porterfield will get the money from the mail clerk, then clear out."

"All right, get the fire lit, then get mounted."

The firewood already having been laid, Michaels dashed a little kerosene onto the pile, then lit it. Within a moment a large fire was burning in the middle of the track.

Boyd McMasters was awakened from a sound sleep by the sudden stopping of the train. He opened his eyes and looked around in the dimly lit car to see what was going on. The other passengers on the train were just as startled by the sudden stop as Boyd, because he heard them talking in confusion. One of the passengers went forward to the vestibule.

There was a heavy, stomach-jarring noise from the front of the train.

"What was that?"

"Sounded like an explosion!"

The passenger who had gone forward, now returned to the car, his eyes wide with fear.

"It's a holdup!" he said, excitedly. "They just blew the door off the mail car, and I seen some men on horses, holdin' guns."

"Oh, my!" one of the women said in a frightened

voice. "Do you think they'll be in here?"

"I don't know, but iffen I was you folks, I'd be hidin' my valuables."

Taking the man's advice, the other passengers quickly began to poke billfolds, coin purses, and jewelry into the various nooks and crannies on the train. They were so distracted by what they were doing that none of them noticed Boyd. He got up slowly and quietly, then eased out the back door. Once outside, he climbed the ladder to the top of the car.

Boyd lay down on roof, using the center ridge not only for concealment but also as a rest for his rifle. He jacked in a shell, then studied the drama playing out before him.

Boyd heard a shot fired from inside the baggage car. That was followed almost immediately by more shots from outside the car, the gun blasts lighting up the darkness with their muzzle flashes.

"No, no, don't shoot no more!" a muffled voice called from inside the car. "You done kilt the guard!"

"Throw out the money pouch, or we'll kill you!" one of the robbers shouted.

Boyd saw the money pouch tossed from the train. He aimed at the robber who was waiting for it, then squeezed off a shot just as the money pouch hit the robber's hands.

The bullet plowed into the robber's chest, raising a little spray of blood which flashed pink against the ambient light of the train and the fire. The robber was knocked from his horse and he lay flat on his back on the ground with both arms spread out to either side. The money pouch lay beside him.

"Deermont!" a voice shouted from the darkness. "Get the money pouch!"

One of the other riders leaned over to pick up the money pouch and Boyd fired a second round. This bullet caught the robber in his elbow, leaving the arm dangling loosely from a few ragged tendons.

"I seen the muzzle flash! He's on the . . ." yelled a third voice.

That was as far as the robber got before another shot from Boyd's big rifle brought him down by blowing a fist-sized hole through his neck.

"Cantrell! We got to get outta here!" another voice shouted, and Boyd watched the unwounded rider, as well as the one with the shattered arm, ride off. Like the fifth, unseen man, the two riders were quickly swallowed up in the darkness. Boyd stood up, hoping he could see them, but he could not. The only evidence of their presence was the sound of hoofbeats, fading in the night.

"We . . . we got to stop!" Deermont shouted.

"We can't stop till we get to Pajarito," Cantrell growled.

"We got to stop. I believe I'm dyin'."

Cantrell reined in his horse, then he looked back at Deermont.

"You just got hit in the arm, didn't you? How you goin' to die from a bullet in the arm?"

"I . . . I don't know," Deermont said.

"Holy shit, Cantrell, look at that arm!" Michaels said.

Cantrell rode back to take a look, then he gasped.

"What is it?" Deermont asked. "What do you see?"

"That arm," Cantrell said. "It looks like you got hit by a cannonball."

Deermont groaned once, then he fell off his horse. Quickly, Michaels hopped down to look at him.

"Did the son of a bitch faint on us?" Cantrell asked.

Michaels examined Deermont more closely for a moment, then he stood up.

"No," he said quietly. "The son of a bitch died on us."

"Died? How the hell could he die from a wound in the arm?"

"This wa'n't no ordinary wound, Cantrell," Michaels said. "I don't know who that was, or what he was shootin', but he pret' near took Deermont's arm clean off. Deermont bled to death."

"Son of a bitch!" Cantrell swore. "Three men killed. Three. And we didn't even get the goddamn money!"

"Who the hell you reckon that was?" Michaels asked. "And what the hell was he shooting?"

"I don't know," Cantrell admitted. "But I ain't lettin' that money get away. Soon as we get to Pajarito, we're roundin' up some more men an' we're goin' after it again."

"Hell, it may be a month before there's another money shipment that big."

"We won't take it off the train," Cantrell said. "We'll take it out of the bank in Crittenden."

"The bank?"

"Yeah. The ten thousand we was going after is peanuts compared to what they keep in the bank. That's where all them rich ranchers are keepin' their money now. There's got to be fifty thousand dollars in there at least."

"We take that bank, we're goin' to have more than a local sheriff after us," Michaels warned. "Any bank that has Cattleman's Association money is protected by the Cattleman's Protective Association, you know that. You want them after us?''

''Don't be worryin' none about them. They got all them banks back in Texas and Kansas and places like that to worry about. They ain't goin' to take no heed of a little bank out here in the Arizona Territory.''

''You don't think so? What about what just happened? Who was that shootin' at us?''

''I figure it was just some passenger on the train,'' Cantrell said. ''It didn't have nothin' at all to do with the Cattleman's Protective Association.''

''Yeah, well, I hope you're right.''

''I am right,'' Cantrell said. ''Come on, let's go to Pajarito.''

Michaels looked at Deermont's body, sprawled on the sand. ''What are we goin' to do about him?'' he asked.

''Nothin'. Leave the son of a bitch for the buzzards,'' Cantrell said. ''Hell, it won't make no difference to him.''

Michaels hesitated for a moment, rubbing his finger on a nose that had been broken so many times that it was almost completely flat. Then he shrugged his shoulders.

''I guess you're right,'' he said. ''It don't matter none to him, now.'' He climbed onto his horse then rode after Cantrell, who had already disappeared into the darkness.

Back at the track it was several more minutes before the train was ready to go again. The train crew discovered that heavy logs had been put on the track just beyond the bonfire, evidence that the rustlers intended to stop the train no matter what it took. While the track was being cleared, the two dead rustlers were picked up and put into the mail car to lie alongside the guard who had also been killed.

Boyd used the time to look around the scene of the crime. He saw a tremendous amount of blood leading off to the south, evidence that the one he had wounded had been wounded badly. Boyd knew that the robber wouldn't survive the night . . . not after losing that much blood. In fact, he wouldn't be surprised if the man wasn't already lying out in the desert somewhere, dead.

Boyd found an empty can with the last couple of beans still fresh. That meant they had waited here for the train long enough for one of them to have his supper. He also found the sign for five horses, though only three of them were carrying weight when they left.

"Hey, mister," the conductor called to him. Boyd looked around. "We're ready to get under way."

Nodding, Boyd started back toward the train.

"I guess it was a lucky thing for us we stopped to pick you up after all," the conductor said, smiling broadly. "That big gun of yours sure came in handy."

Three

The town of Crittenden was divided into two sections. There was the American section, which lay to the north of the track, and the Mexican section, which lay to the south. Though many towns in this part of the territory were more Mexican than American, Crittenden had a somewhat heavier American flavor, due to the fact that it was situated on a loop of the Southern Pacific Railroad.

Like most towns along the network of railroads that covered the West, the lifeline of the community was the tracks, and its heartbeat the daily arrival and departure of the trains. Trains brought newspapers and goods from far-off places, providing tiny Crittenden with a real and visible link to the rest of the country. All the trains, especially those that arrived at night, caused a large and enthusiastic turnout of the townspeople, American and Mexican alike.

There was always a carnival atmosphere about the crowd, with laughter and good-natured joking. From the Mexicans there would often be strumming guitars and clattering maracas. The crowd would begin to gather at the depot about half an hour before the train was due to arrive, growing with each passing minute until, at the appointed hour, there would be two score or more on hand. Then would come the high point of the evening, the arrival of the engine. The whistle could be heard first, far off and mournful.

"Here she comes!" someone would shout, and the laughter and talking and the music would stop as if everyone were consciously giving the approaching train center stage.

The first thing to come into view would be the light, a huge, wavering, yellow disk, the gas flame and mirror reflector shining brightly in the distance. The sighting would be closely followed by the hollow sounds of puffing steam, then the glowing sparks which were whipped away in the black smoke clouds that billowed up into the night sky. Finally the engine would rush by with white wisps of steam escaping from the thrusting piston rods, sparks flying from the pounding drive wheels, and glowing hot embers dripping from the fire box. Then would come the yellow squares of light that were the windows of the passenger cars, slowing, and finally grinding to a halt with a shower of sparks and a hissing of air from the Westinghouse air brakes.

"Look!" someone shouted. "Look at the door on the mail car! It looks like it's been blowed off!"

The arriving passengers began to detrain then, met by family and friends. Very quickly after that the stories they carried were repeated throughout the crowd, even among those who were meeting no one.

"Did you hear? Someone tried to hold up the train!"

"Tried? You mean they didn't get away with it?"

"Nope. Two of 'em was shot down and the others got away without the money."

"Sounds like the guard the bank hired earned his money."

"The guard hell. He got hisself kilt. It was one of the passengers that shot 'am."

Sheriff Emil Lindsey and his deputy, Harley Gibbons, were pushing their way through the crowd toward the mail car.

"Get back," Harley was saying. "Get back, ever'body. Make way! Let me an' the sheriff through here!"

Dooley, the mail clerk, climbed down from the train. He had a bandage wrapped around his head, covering the wound he received when the door was blown.

"What happened here, Dooley?" Sheriff Lindsey asked.

"Someone tried to rob us, Sheriff," Dooley said. "Poor old Cartright got hisself killed tryin' to fight 'em off."

"Did they get the money?" an overweight, middle-aged man asked, pushing through the crowd. This was Richard Adams, the banker.

"No sir, Mr. Adams," Dooley said, proudly. "The money pouch is safe."

"We got three bodies on board, Sheriff," the conductor said. "What do you want to do with 'em?"

"One of 'em Cartright?"

"Yes, sir."

"I'll send a telegram back to the sheriff in Tombstone. He can tell Cartright's family. Who are the other two?"

"They are a couple of the galoots that tried to rob us," the conductor said.

Sheriff Lindsey turned to his deputy. "Harley, get 'em

out of the car and lay 'em on the platform,'' he said. ''Let's take a look at 'em.''

Soliciting help from a couple of men in the crowd, Harley soon had the two bodies out on the wooden loading platform. Sheriff Lindsey, leaning down and holding a lantern over their faces, examined them carefully. The crowd moved in for a closer look, with many of the Mexicans crossing themselves as they did so.

''Hey, Emil, I know them two boys,'' Harley said. ''That's Porterfield and Slater. They used to cowboy some for the Bar T.''

''Yeah, I know them, too,'' Sheriff Lindsey said. He pointed to the one with the wound in his chest. ''This is Marcus Porterfield. The other one is Dan Slater. If you recollect, we've had 'em both in jail more than once.''

''I do recollect,'' Harley said. ''And now that I think on it, it'd be just like them boys to try 'n hold up a train. They always was lookin' for some way to get aroun' workin'.''

''Don't reckon either one of 'em will have to be worryin' 'bout work now,'' Lindsey said.

''What the hell?'' Lindsey asked, just noticing the size of the bullet hole. He put his fingers on Porterfield's chest and looked more closely at the wound.

''I'll be damned!'' he said. ''Would you look at the size of that hole, Harley? What kind of gun would make a wound like that?'' He looked back up at the conductor. ''Who did you say shot them?''

''It was one of the passengers,'' the conductor said.

''He was shootin' from up on the roof of our car,'' a passenger from the train added. ''Sounded like he was shootin' a cannon.''

"Looks like he was shootin' one, too," Harley said. "Look here, Emil. I could damn near put my hand in ol' Porterfield's chest and pull his heart out."

"Who are you kiddin'?" someone in the crowd asked. "I know'd Porterfield, an' the son of a bitch didn't have no heart."

Several of the others laughed nervously.

"I saw the rifle he was shooting," the conducter said. "It was one he said he made himself. The fella told me it was a .70-caliber."

"A .70-caliber?" Lindsey whistled softly. "That's bigger than two .32s put together."

"I'll say," the conductor said. "I've seen lots of guns in my day, but I tell you, I have never seen a gun that big."

The sheriff straightened up, then looked up and down the platform. Most of those who had come to meet the train, as well as the passengers who had arrived and those who were still on the train, were gathered around for a closer view of the grisly sight. The women were holding handkerchiefs over their noses, though that was more symbolic than anything else, for the men had been too recently killed for their bodies to be ripe. The men were somewhat bolder, though Sheriff Lindsey noticed that the expressions in the faces of more than a few of them showed that, like the women, their stomachs were just a little queasy.

"Which one of the passengers did this?" the sheriff asked.

"He's right over . . ." the conductor started, then he paused. "That's funny. He was there a moment ago; I saw him gettin' off the train. Where did he go?"

"What did he look like?" Sheriff Lindsey asked.

"He was a tall fella. Dark hair, brown eyes," the conductor replied. " 'Bout thirty or so, I reckon." The conductor pulled out his watch and looked at it. "Listen, Sheriff, I got to get goin'. We got a schedule to meet. You need me for anything else?"

"No," Lindsey said. "I reckon not."

"Board!" the conductor shouted, and there was a flurry of activity as several of the through passengers who had left to check out the excitement, now hurried back to the train to resume their trip.

"Make certain he doesn't get back on and get away," Lindsey said. "I'd sure like to talk to the fella who shot these two varmints."

"I seen him goin' into the depot," someone from the crowd said.

"Thanks."

Sheriff Lindsey and his deputy went into the depot to have a look around. When they saw no one there who answered the description the conductor had given them, Lindsey asked the man behind the baggage counter if he had seen him.

"Sounds like the fella that dropped off that saddle over there."

"You got any idea where he went?"

"Asked me where he could get 'im a bath and a room. I told 'im the Dunnigan Hotel."

Sheriff Lindsey stroked his chin and looked down toward the hotel. "Bath and a room, huh? Well, that don't sound like he's aimin' to run off anywhere, does it? And I reckon he's earned himself that. I'll just give him time to get settled in before I look him up."

•   •   •

"Yes, sir." The desk clerk at the Dunnigan Hotel was
replying to Boyd's question at that very moment. "We
got the latest in bathing rooms. There's two of 'em down
at the end of the hall up on the second floor. All you
got to do is start the fire in the water heater, give it a
few minutes to heat up, then turn the spigot. Before you
know it you'll have a whole tub full of hot water."

"Thanks."

Boyd took the key to his room upstairs. Before he
went to his room he walked down to the end of the hall
to one of the bathing rooms. He went into one and
started a fire in the water heater. Then he walked down
to check out his room while he gave the water time to
warm up.

It was an adequate room. He would certainly be more
comfortable here than he was on the frequent nights he
spent out on the trail. On the other hand the room was
a poor substitute for the house he had built for his Hannah . . . the house that was torched by outlaws. Boyd lost
his wife, his house, and his ranch on that terrible day.

Boyd did exact his revenge. The outlaws who killed
his wife and burned his house were the Winslow brothers. Boyd killed every Winslow, but the satisfaction of
that blood-lust did nothing to fill the vast emptiness that
was left in his heart. Now he was always looking down
the road, over the next hill, past the fork in the
road . . . searching for something he couldn't put a name
to. But, no matter how much he wandered, no matter
how much he searched, the pain of his loss was always
just a thought away.

Boyd pinched the bridge of his nose to force back
those terrible memories. He knew he could never make
them completely go away . . . they were always there,

just beneath the surface of his consciousness. They were at the soul of his very being. Even the icy coolness for which he was known came from the fact that he had already lost his reason for living. He was now so detached from life that he was absolutely without fear. He literally didn't care whether he lived or died.

Boyd walked over to look out the window. From here he had a good view of the main street. The street, scarred with wagon ruts and dotted with horse droppings, formed an "X" with the track. The railroad station was halfway down the street and he saw that the train he had arrived on was just now pulling away. On the far side of the track he saw a scattering of adobe buildings. On this side of the track the buildings were false-fronted and made of unpainted, rip-sawed lumber. Right across the street from the hotel was the livery stable. Below him and next door to the hotel was the Second Chance Saloon.

Because the saloon was under him, he couldn't actually see it from his window, but he could see the bright splash of light it threw into the street, and he could hear laughter and piano music.

That was for him. After he had his bath, he would go downstairs and have his supper, then go into the saloon to see if he could find a poker game. Poker was one of his few diversions. It helped get him through another day and, ever since Hannah died, all he could ask for was that he get through one more day.

He left the room and walked down to the end of the hall to take his bath.

The woman was just getting into the tub when Boyd opened the door. She stood there for a moment, so surprised by his unexpected appearance that she made no effort to cover herself. She was totally nude, and Boyd breathed in a quick gasp of appreciation for her beauty.

"Sir, as you can readily see, this room is occupied," the woman said calmly.

Boyd smiled. "Yes, ma'am, I do see," he replied. "I'm sorry, I had built the fire for my own bath, but I see you beat me to it." He stared pointedly at the woman's nudity and, as if realizing for the first time that she was naked, the woman took in a sharp breath, then sat down in the water so quickly that she raised a splash.

"You should have knocked," she said.

"You should have locked," he replied.

"But, I did lock the door," the woman said, pointing to a door at the rear of the room. "I always come through that door. I didn't realize this door had been unlocked."

"No harm done," Boyd said. "There's another bathing room next door. I'll use it."

"Yes, thank you, I believe that would be most appropriate."

Forty-five minutes later, bathed and shaved, Boyd went into the dining room downstairs, only to learn that it was too late to eat because the kitchen was closed for the night.

"You got any idea where I could go to get something to eat?" Boyd asked.

"There are a couple of beaneries that stay open all night over in Mex-town," the maitre d' said. "Or you might try next door at the saloon. They serve an adequate if somewhat limited menu," he said haughtily.

"Thanks," Boyd replied. Leaving the hotel, he

walked next door, then pushed through the batwing doors of the Second Chance Saloon. There were half a dozen filled tables, though he didn't see a game going on at any of them. Disappointed, he stepped up to the bar to order a whiskey.

"The drink is on me, Marty," a voice said from behind Boyd as the bartender poured the glass. When Boyd turned around he saw a middle-aged man wearing a sheriff's badge. The sheriff stuck out his hand. "I'm Emil Lindsey. I'm the sheriff here. Unless I miss my guess, you're the one who killed the two train robbers."

"Three," Boyd said easily, taking the sheriff's hand.

"Three? Only two were brought in."

"I wounded one and he rode off," Boyd said. "By now, he's dead."

"Gutshot?"

"Nope. I hit him in the arm."

"Arm? You wounded one in the arm and you think he'll die?"

"I know he'll die. They don't recover from the wounds I give them," Boyd said.

Sheriff Lindsey stroked his chin for a moment as he studied the young man before him.

"Yes, the conductor did tell me about that rifle of yours. Seventy-caliber I believe he said. And you made it yourself?"

"I did. It's based on the Sharps rifles used by Berdan's marksmen during the War Between the States. There are some big differences, though. The ones they used were .52-caliber . . . and as you've already noted, I've bored mine out to be a .70. Also, their guns shot only once, whereas I've changed the barrel and receiver assembly to convert mine into a lever-action repeater."

"Why would an ordinary citizen need a gun like that?" Lindsey asked.

"I don't know that an ordinary citizen would. I use it in my business."

Lindsey's eyes narrowed. "I see. You wouldn't be a bounty hunter, would you, Mister . . ."

"McMasters. Boyd McMasters."

The challenging expression left Lindsey's face and he smiled, broadly. "McMasters? Yes, of course, you are *Cap'n* McMasters, from the Cattleman's Protective Association," he said. "We've been expecting you, Cap'n. Or at least, Richard Adams has. He owns the bank here, and he's most anxious to get the Association's endorsement. As a matter of fact you might be interested in knowing that the money you saved tonight was a cash transfer from the bank in Tombstone to cover a draft deposited by one of the larger depositors."

"Excuse me, Sheriff Lindsey?" a small, thin man asked, coming into the saloon at that moment.

"Yes."

"This telegram just arrived. It's addressed to a Captain Boyd McMasters in care of you," the man said. "Would you be knowing such a person?"

The sheriff smiled. "You're standing right in front of the gentleman," he said, nodding toward Boyd.

"Then I suppose this must be for you," the man said, handing Boyd the envelope.

"Thanks," Boyd replied, giving the man a nickel. He tore open the envelope and pulled out the message.

CAPTAIN BOYD MCMASTERS
C/O SHERIFF'S OFFICE
CRITTENDEN ARIZ TER

THIS TO INFORM YOU DOBBS BROTHERS ESCAPED
JAIL THREE DAYS AGO STOP KILLED DEPUTY
SIMMONS AND JUDGE BOGGS STOP DOBBS BELIEVED
HEADED INTO ARIZ TER STOP CASE ASSIGNED TO
ANOTHER AGENT BUT YOU ARE TO BE ON LOOKOUT
STOP

BORDEN MCMASTERS

"Damn," Boyd said, pinching the bridge of his nose.
He handed the telegram to Sheriff Lindsey.

"The Dobbs brothers, yes, I read about them. They
murdered a ranch family?"

"After they raped the wife and daughter, yes," Boyd
said.

Lindsey snapped his fingers. "Now that I recall,
you're the one who caught them, aren't you? You killed
the Andersons and captured the Dobbses."

"I did."

"And now the Dobbses are on the loose again. Too
bad. You should've killed them as well."

"Yes, I should have," Boyd said simply.

"Well, they're not your worry now. Like the telegram
says, someone else has been assigned to their case. Listen, did I hear you say you were looking for supper?"

"I am. It's too late for the hotel dining room."

"Do you like steak?"

"I'd be in the wrong business if I didn't," Boyd replied.

"Marty," Lindsey called to the bartender. "Fix Cap'n
McMasters a steak, and fry him up some potatoes and
give him a side of beans. Charge it to my office."

"Sure thing, Sheriff."

"That takes care of supper," Boyd said. "Now, if I

could only find myself a good poker game."

"What about Sam's game?" Marty asked the sheriff.

"Sam's game?" Boyd asked. "Is it a good game?"

"It's a good game," the sheriff replied. "But you can't come to the table with less than fifty dollars worth of chips."

"That's all right, if it's an honest game."

"Oh, it's honest, all right. Sam wouldn't have it any other way," Lindsey said. He looked at the pistols Boyd was wearing. "But you'll have to check your guns with Marty before you play."

"That Sam's rule?"

"My rule," Lindsey answered. "I don't want anyone gettin' killed in my town over a card game. Even a high-stakes game."

"All right," Boyd said. "If everyone else has checked their guns, I guess I can check mine, too."

"Good luck in your game," Lindsey said, touching the brim of his hat.

"Thanks. And thanks for the drink and the vittles."

Two drinks and one cigarillo later, Marty brought Boyd a steak that was so large it spilled over the edge of his plate. There were potatoes, too, fried with onions and bell peppers, and a steaming bowl of beans, seasoned with pork and hot peppers.

Boyd was a slim man, the kind many called wiry. But he was a man who enjoyed eating. He was also a man whose natural level of energy and body activity was such that he could eat a meal this large with no appreciable gain of weight. And he so often ate jerky, or wild game while on the trail that he truly enjoyed, and took advantage of, any opportunity to eat well. Tonight was just such an opportunity.

He washed it all down with beer, then, pushing his empty plate aside, signaled for Marty.

"Marty, I'm ready for the game," he said.

Marty held out his hand. "Give me your guns."

Boyd took the his gun belt off and handed it to Marty. Marty walked over to put it under the bar, then he curled his finger as a signal for Boyd to follow him.

They went into a small alcove off the back of the saloon. Boyd smiled. This was what he had been looking for. Here was a large, round table, covered with green felt, surrounded by comfortable chairs. There were three men at the table and there was one empty chair. At first he thought they were playing a small, three-handed game, then he saw that they weren't playing at all, but were waiting for a fourth person who was away from the table. Boyd knew there was a fourth person by the stack of chips in front of that chair. That stack was higher than any of the other stacks.

"Fellas, this here is Cap'n McMasters," Marty said by way of introduction. "He's come to play poker."

"Captain?" one of the players said.

"He's a captain in the Cattleman's Protective Association."

"You the fella Richard Adams has been waitin' to see?" one of the players asked.

"I guess I am."

The questioner chuckled. "He's been gettin' ready for you for two weeks. Brought in that new safe, put bars on the windows. I guess gettin' a good report from you fellas is pretty important."

"We like to think so," Boyd said.

"There's an extra chair over there. Pull it over here and sit in."

"Wait a minute," one of the other players said, quickly. "Before you bring over the chair tell me, Captain, how much do you make in that job of yours?" This was a fat man with heavy jowls and narrow squinting eyes. He was wearing a tan jacket and a dark brown silk vest. A gold chain stretched across his vest, accenting his girth.

"Why do you ask?" Boyd retorted.

"The reason I ask . . . Captain . . . is because this isn't a penny-ante game. In fact you might find something more to your liking out there." He nodded toward the main area of the saloon.

"There aren't any games out there," Boyd said.

"Too bad."

"Hold on there, Angus, you got no call to be rude," the one who had invited Boyd to pull up a chair said. He was a man in his early sixties, wearing a dark blue suit. He also had gray hair and whiskers and friendly eyes. He looked over at Boyd. "What he is saying, friend, is that you have to buy a minimum of fifty dollars worth of chips to get into the game. If you can do that, you're more than welcome at our table."

"The sheriff explained the rules," Boyd said. "I'll take a hundred." He took five gold double-eagles from his pocket and put them on the table in front of him.

"Pete, you're the banker tonight, aren't you?" the gray-haired man asked. "Take care of our new player."

Pete was about thirty, slim and clean-shaven, with a hawk-like nose. Like Boyd, Pete wasn't wearing a suit. He reached over into the chip box and took out a handful of painted chips, in red, white, and blue. "Red is one, white is five and blue is ten," he explained, sliding the appropriate amount over to Boyd.

"I'm Ben Taylor," the gray haired man said. "I'm also the dentist here 'bouts, so most folks call me Doc. The man handing you the chips is Pete Mallory, and the large gentleman with the suspiscious attitude is Angus Waddle. Pete runs the livery stable and Angus owns the general store."

"Where's Sam? I thought this was his game."

"His game?" Doc asked. He laughed, then turned his head. "Sam? Sam, we've got a new player."

A door to the side of the alcove opened and the absent player came in.

"Captain McMasters, meet Sam," Doc said.

Sam turned out to be a beautiful young woman. She was wearing a beaded green dress which clung to her figure and dipped low enough to show the tops of her breasts. Sometimes, Boyd knew, such dresses were designed to push and shape breasts, promising more than was there. That wasn't the case with Sam, however. Everything this dress promised was, indeed, there. Boyd knew that for a fact, for this was the same woman he had seen just stepping into the bathtub, earlier this evening.

"Good evening, Captain McMasters," Sam said, smiling at him. "How was your bath?"

"Fine," Boyd answered. "How was yours?"

"It was quite pleasant once I got rid of the draft," she teased. She took her seat. "Shall we play a little cards?"

Four

"New player, new deck," Sam said. She picked up a box, broke the seal, then dumped the cards onto the table. They were clean, stiff, and shining. She pulled out the joker then began shuffling the deck. The stiff new pasteboards clicked sharply. Her hands moved swiftly, folding the cards in and out until the law of random numbers became king. She shoved the deck across the table.

"Cut?" she invited Boyd. She leaned over the table, showing a generous amount of cleavage.

Boyd cut the deck, then pushed them back. He tried to focus on her hands, though it was difficult to do so because she kept finding ways to position herself to draw his eyes toward her more interesting parts.

"You aren't having trouble concentrating, are you, Captain McMasters?" Sam teased.

"No," Boyd replied. He smiled. "If I need more than you are showing me, all I have to do is think back a mite. I can recall everything I saw in great detail."

"You naughty boy. I believe you had all the fun."

"I'm beginnin' to think that you enjoyed it some more than you let on," Boyd challenged.

"Perhaps that is true," Sam admitted with a twinkle in her eyes.

"Here, what's goin' on here?" Angus asked. "You two know each other?"

"Not yet," Sam answered. She licked her lips. "But I have a feeling we are going to. Five card?" She paused before she said the next word. "Stud?"

"Fine," Boyd answered.

Boyd won fifteen dollars on the first hand, and a couple of hands later he was ahead by a little over thirty dollars. The other players were taking Boyd's good luck in stride, but Angus Waddle began complaining.

"Somethin' kinda fishy is goin' on here," he said.

"Fishy, Angus?" Sam replied sweetly.

Angus looked at Sam, then nodded toward Boyd. "You're dealin' him winnin' hands," he said.

"How can you say that?" Sam replied. "The deal has passed around the table and Captain McMasters has been winning, no matter who is dealing."

"Are you trying to tell me his winnin' is just dumb luck?"

"No, it's not just luck, and there's nothing dumb about it," Boyd said. "There's a degree of skill involved in knowing when to hold and when to fold. You obviously haven't learned that."

"Is that a fact?" Angus said. He stared across the table through narrowed eyes. "Suppose you and I have a go by ourselves? Showdown for twenty-five dollars."

"Showdown?" Boyd chuckled. "All right, I see you're trying to even up the odds a bit by taking the skill out. But I'll go with you."

Angus reached for the cards but Boyd stuck his hand out to stop him. "You don't think I'm going to let you deal, do you? We'll let the lady deal.''

"Uh, uh,'' Angus said, shaking his head. He nodded toward Pete Mallory. "We'll let Pete deal.''

"How do I know that you and Pete aren't in cahoots? Suppose we let Doc deal,'' Boyd suggested.

"Agreed.''

Doc dealt five cards to each of them. Boyd took the pot with a pair of twos.

Angus laughed. "Not exactly a smashing hand, was it? How about another?''

Boyd won that hand with a jack high.

"Want another one?'' Boyd asked.

"Yes,'' Angus replied. "You can't possibly win three in a row.''

Boyd did win the third, with a pair of tens and Angus threw his cards on the table in disgust. He slid the rest of his money to the center of the table. "I've thirty-six dollars here,'' he said. "High card.''

Boyd covered his bet, then Doc fanned the cards out.

"You draw first,'' Angus said.

Boyd started to reach for a card, but just as he touched it, Angus stopped him. "No, I changed my mind,'' he said. "I'll draw first.'' Angus smiled triumphantly, then flipped over the card Boyd was about to draw. It was a three of hearts.

"What the . . .'' Angus shouted in anger. "You cheated me, you son of a bitch! You knew I was going to do that so you reached for the low card!''

"How was I supposed to know that was a low card?'' Boyd asked. "The cards are facedown on the table.'' Boyd turned over a seven of diamonds, then reached for the chips.

Angus reached inside his jacket and pulled out a

"pepper-box," a small, palm-sized pistol.

"Mister, cheaters don't get away with it in this town. I'll thank you to slide that money back across the table," he said.

"Angus!" Sam gasped. "He wasn't cheating! And what are you doing with that pistol? You know no one is supposed to be armed in here!"

Angus smiled. "Yeah, I know," he said. "That sort of gives me the advantage, doesn't it?" He motioned with his other hand. "Push the money over here to me."

"Oh, do you mean I was supposed to have checked my gun somewhere?" Boyd asked.

"Yes," Sam said. "There's a strict rule about that."

"Sorry," Boyd said. "I didn't know that. I guess that's why I've got a Colt .44 pointing at this man's belly."

Angus started to sweat and his hand began to shake.

"No, you don't," he said. "All the guns are supposed to be checked."

"Oh, but I do, Angus." From under the table came a distinct sound, like the sound of a .44 being cocked. "And mine's already cocked," he added, calling attention to the fact that the hammer had not yet been pulled back on Angus's pepper-box gun.

Angus moved his thumb toward the hammer.

"I wouldn't do that," Boyd cautioned, smiling, and shaking his head slowly. "You start to come back on that hammer and I'll blow a hole in your belly big enough to stick my fist into."

Slowly, and with a trembling hand, Angus put the pistol down on the table. Boyd reached over to pick it up, then he handed it to Sam.

"Break it open and empty the charges," he said.

Sam pushed the hinged barrel down, then shook out all the cartridges.

"Now, perhaps we can get on with our game," Boyd suggested, and he brought his other hand up to the top of the table. He was holding a pocket knife. With his thumb, he flipped the blade open and closed, making a sound exactly like that of a .44 being cocked.

"You . . . you didn't even have a gun!" Angus sputtered, angrily.

"Like you said, all the guns had to be checked," Boyd replied innocently. Everyone laughed.

Angus stood up and pointed at Boyd.

"One of these days mister, you're going to try something like that and it's going to blow up right in your face."

"I suppose there is always that chance," Boyd agreed. "But then, that's what makes life worth livin'."

When Boyd went to bed that night he rolled his poker winnings into a tight roll, then stuck the money into the pillowcase. After that he extinguished the lantern, shucked out of his boots, pants, and shirt, and climbed into bed. It had been six days since he slept in a real bed, and the springs, mattress, and almost-clean sheets felt very good to him.

Boyd opened his eyes. Something had awakened him, and he lay very still. The doorknob turned and Boyd was up, reaching for the gun that lay on a table by his bed. He moved as quietly as a cat, stepping to the side of the door and cocking his Colt .44. Naked, except for a pair of skivvies, he felt the night air on his skin. His senses were alert, his body alive with readiness.

Boyd could hear someone breathing on the other side of the door. A thin shaft of hall light shone underneath. Outside the hotel he heard a tinkling piano and a burst of laughter. From the other side of the track came the high-pitched bleat of a trumpet. He took a deep breath and smelled lilacs, then he smiled. He had smelled this same perfume earlier.

"Sam?" he called.

"Are you awake?" the visitor replied.

Like the scent, the voice belonged to Sam. It was low and husky, with just a hint of rawness to it.

Boyd eased the hammer down on the pistol, then opened the door to let a wide bar of light spill into the room. Sam stood in the doorway. The hall lantern was backlighting the thin cotton robe she was wearing, and he could see her body in shadow behind the cloth. It was easy to see that she was wearing nothing underneath.

"Come on in," Boyd invited, moving back to let her step inside. He closed the door, then crossed over to light the lantern on his table. A bubble of light illuminated the room.

"Oh, my. You aren't wearing much, are you?" Sam said, seeing Boyd in his skivvies.

"If you want, I'll get dressed."

"Why bother?" Sam asked. "You'll just have to get undressed again." Crossing over to him, she put her arms around his neck and pulled him to her for a kiss. She pressed her body hard against him, then opened her mouth hungrily to seek out his tongue. Boyd's arms wound around her tightly and he felt the heat of her body transferring itself to his own body. She ground herself against him and his blood changed to hot whiskey.

"Oh," Sam said throatily, as she felt Boyd's erection

pushing against her. "Is that for me? All for me?" She stepped back from him, then opened her robe and let it fall from her shoulders. As he had already surmised, she was nude underneath, and her body shined golden in the soft light from the table lantern. "I thought I would give you another look, just in case you forgot everything you saw this afternoon."

"I'm not likely to forget," Boyd said. "But I'll enjoy another look."

Sam reached for Boyd's skivvies. "What about me?" she asked. "Don't I get a look, too?"

With Sam's help, Boyd slipped out of his skivvies, then stood before her, as naked as she.

"Do you want me to turn out the lantern?"

"No," Sam answered. "I want to look at you while we are doing it."

They moved over to the iron-stead bed. The covers were already turned back and the springs squealed in protest as Boyd sat down.

"The bed squeaks," Boyd noted.

"Good," Sam replied, putting her arms around his neck, then pushing him back on the bed and crawling on top of him. "I want us to play a concert."

Sam straddled him as if she were riding a horse, then reaching down, she guided him into her hot, wet cleft. With her eyes closed, she leaned forward, biting her lips in the ecstasy of the moment.

Boyd's mouth was dry and he could feel the blood pounding in his temples as he ran his hands over her shoulders, then across her firm, nipple-crowned breasts. Sam began moving up and down on him, her motion starting the bed to squeak.

"No," Boyd said after a moment.

"No? What do you mean, no?" Sam gasped.

Boyd smiled, then reached for her shoulders. "I want to be on top," he explained.

"Get on top if you must," Sam replied, "but if you break the connection I'll scratch your eyes out."

Laughing, Boyd put his hands on her hips, then he lifted himself up and flipped over, keeping her impaled by his hard shaft.

"Oh!" she said. "Oh, my, that is good!"

With Sam on the bottom now, Boyd lifted her legs until her heels were on his shoulders. Then he thrust deep into her, driving himself in as far as he could go.

Grunting and moaning with pleasure, she thrashed about on a bed which was now squeaking loudly in accompaniment to her whimpering barks. She reached up to put her arms around his neck and, tilting her head back into the pillow, bucked against him to meet each of his sensory-laden thrusts.

Boyd grabbed her buttocks with his hands, holding her to him as, again and again he thrust into her. He looked at her face and saw her lips pulled back against her pearl-white teeth, a grimace, not unlike one in pain, though he knew this was of pure pleasure.

He continued to pump away for several moments, finding in her and the resilient, though dissonant springs, a perfect cushion for his thrusts. She moaned and groaned and thrashed beneath him, sometimes shuddering in uncontrollable spasms. Not wanting to finish too quickly, he slowed his movements and began pulling away as she bucked against him.

"No" she moaned. "What are you doing? Don't stop!"

"I'm holding back for you," Boyd said.

"Honey, don't you know?" Sam gasped through clenched teeth. "I've already done it twice! Do it. Do it, damn you! I want to feel you spraying inside me!"

Sam augmented her demands with another forceful buck, and the feel of her movements and the eroticism of her words broke down the last bit of willpower Boyd had. He rammed full-force once again, deep into her, slamming her against the bed, bouncing back with the squeaking symphony of the springs, speeding headlong toward the conclusion with no intention now of slowing or pulling back. He saw her tightly drawn nipples atop jiggling, sweat-patinaed breasts . . . saw her teeth nibbling at her bottom lip, heard her cry out one more time, then felt her spasmatic orgasm bring about his own release. He spewed forth in a hot gushing blast, pounding and thrusting as, time after time the waves of muscular contractions swept up from the soles of his feet, down from his scalp, around from the middle of his back, and deep from within his gut, finally spending itself through a penis that, even as it began to relax, continued to throb with sensation.

Boyd collapsed across Sam, breathing heavily as he coasted down from the pinnacle. Finally he flopped over to lie beside her.

"Oh, honey, I knew you would be good," Sam said, breathlessly.

Boyd reached over to put his hand on her naked hip. He let it slide over until it reached the cushion of hair over the wet cleft between her legs. He chuckled.

"What is it? What's funny?" she asked.

"First time I ever did this with someone named Sam."

She laughed with him.

"I must say, you don't feel like a Sam," he added.

"Actually, it's Samantha. Samantha Chance."

"Samantha. It's a pretty name. Why do you call yourself Sam?"

"I'm a professional gambler," Sam explained. "Using the name Sam sometimes gives me an advantage." She reached over to give his now inert penis one last squeeze, then she sat up.

"Where are you going?" Boyd asked.

"Back to my own room."

"You don't have to. You could stay the night, leave in the morning."

Sam leaned over to kiss Boyd on his forehead. "Captain McMasters, I came in here for you to make love to me, not marry me," she explained.

Boyd chuckled. "Okay, we won't get married. But haven't we gone a little beyond you calling me Captain McMasters? My name is Boyd."

"Boyd, I wouldn't want anyone to see me coming out of your room tomorrow. I don't want to give anyone the wrong idea."

"The wrong idea?"

"I am a woman alone. My business is conducted in saloons. It would be easy for someone to misunderstand . . . for someone to think that I was 'on-the-line.' But I am not a whore and I never have been. As far as the men around here are concerned, I am unapproachable. That's what they think and that's what I want them to think.

"Of course, you may think my coming to your room tonight belies that. It must seem like a bold thing to do, perhaps even a slatternly thing to do. But it's all a part of my plan. You see, I made up my mind, long ago, that

I would decide when and I would decide with whom I would make love. That way, I am in control. Do you understand that?"

Boyd chuckled, softly. "I not only understand it, I appreciate it."

"And you'll keep this our little secret?"

"Wild horses won't drag it out of me," Boyd promised.

Five

Cantrell and Michaels reached the tiny town of Pajarito just after midnight. Tired and frustrated over the botched train robbery, Cantrell bought a bottle of tequilla at the cantina, then picked up a Mexican whore, taking her as much for her bed as for any of the "special" services she could provide for him.

Pajarito was a scattering of fly-blown, crumbling adobe buildings laid out around a dusty plaza. It was twenty miles south of where the attempted train robbery had taken place. What made Pajarito attractive to people like Jason Cantrell was its reputation as a "Robbers' Roost" or "Outlaw Haven."

The town had no constable or sheriff, and visitations by law officers from elsewhere in the territory were strongly discouraged. There was a place in the town cemetery prominently marked as "Lawman's Plot." Here, two deputy sheriffs, one deputy U.S. Marshal, a private detective, and an Arizona Ranger—all uninvited visitors to the the town—lay buried.

Cantrell woke up the next morning with a ravenous hunger and a raging need to urinate. The *puta* was still asleep beside him. She had the bedcover askew, exposing one enormous, pillow-sized, heavily blue-veined breast. One fat leg dangled over the edge of the bed. She was snoring loudly and a bit of spittle drooled from her vibrating lips. She didn't wake up when Cantrell crawled over her to get out of bed and get dressed.

There was an outhouse twenty feet behind the little adobe crib, but Cantrell disdained its use, going against the wall instead.

"Michaels," he called as he stood there, relieving himself. "Michaels, you still in there?"

Michaels had gone with the *puta* in the next crib over. Cantrell heard a sound from within the shadows of the crib, then Michaels appeared in the doorway. He was wearing his boots, hat, and longjohns. He joined Cantrell at the wall.

"I want you to round up three good men," Cantrell said as they stood their relieving themselves. He shook himself, then put it away. "I'm goin' over to have breakfast. Bring 'em there."

"We goin' after that bank in Crittenden?"

"Yeah," Cantrell said. "We're goin' after that bank in Crittenden."

In the Casa del Sol cantina, Cantrell rolled a tortilla in his fingers and, using it like a spoon, scooped up the last of his breakfast beans. He washed it down with a drink of coffee, then lit a cigar as Michaels came over to his table, leading three men.

"Here they are, Cantrell. I got us three good men, just like you said."

Cantrell looked at the three, then he frowned. "That one's a Mex," he said. The Mexican had obsidian eyes, a dark brooding face, and a black moustache which curved down around either side of his mouth. He was wearing an oversized sombrero. "I don't work with Mexicans."

"Paco's a good man," Michaels insisted.

"How do you know?"

"Me an' him have done a couple of jobs together," Michaels said. He chuckled. "Besides, you slept with his sister last night."

Cantrell took a puff of his cigar, then squinted through the smoke. "Well, if you come along . . . Paco . . . you only get half a share," he said, setting the Mexican's name apart from the rest of the sentence.

Without a word, Paco turned and started to walk away.

"Wait a minute," Cantrell called to him.

"For half a share, *señor*, I don't do shit," Paco said. It sounded like "sheet."

Cantrell laughed. "If you can't be bought off that easy, you might do."

Paco came back to the table.

"What will you do for a full share?" Cantreall asked.

"Anything you say."

"There might be some killin'," Cantrell suggested.

"I do not want to be the one who is killed," the Mexican said. "But if I am the one doing the killing, it is okay."

"You're in."

The other two didn't have to undergo the same degree of interrogation because Cantrell knew them and had worked with them before. They were the Dobbs brothers, Curly and Frank. Curly might have had curly hair at one time, but he was now totally bald. He was also short and wide, with powerful shoulders and no neck, so that he somewhat resembled a cannonball. Frank, on the other hand, was tall and thin. They bore little resemblance to each other, for all that they were brothers.

"What you got in mind?" Curly asked.

"Money," Cantrell answered without being more specific. "I've got money in mind."

"How much money?" Frank asked. He was holding a judge's gavel, which he kept tapping into the palm of his left hand.

Cantrell studied them through his half-drooped left eye. "A lot of money," he finally answered. "All the rich cattlemen in Pima County have put their money in the bank in Crittenden. If you was to take all the money the five of us have ever had, and put it in one pile, it wouldn't make as much as one share of the money that's in that bank now. Are you fellas interested?"

Curly smiled. "Hell, yes, I'm interested."

"Me, too," Frank added. He continued to play with the gavel.

"What about your cousins?" Cantrell asked.

"What's their names? Matt and Luke? Think they'd want in on this?"

"I reckon they would if they was still alive," Curly said. "But they got themselves killed here a few weeks back."

"Too bad," Cantrell said. "They was good men."

"When do we go after it?" Frank asked.

"Couple more days," Cantrell replied. "When I think it's the right time."

By the next day, news of the aborted train robbery had spread all over Pajarito. At the cantina, one man, who had just come from Crittenden, was anxious to tell everyone else about the man who had broken up the robbery.

"His name is Boyd McMasters, and he is a Captain in the Cattleman's Protective Association."

"McMasters?" Curly said with a quick intake of breath. "What the hell is he doin' in Crittenden?"

"They say he was comin' to check out the bank they got there. But he just happened to be on the train because his horse broke a leg and McMasters hitched a ride."

"You know this man, McMasters?" Cantrell asked the Dobbs brothers.

"Yeah, we know 'im," Curly said. "We know the son of a bitch too well."

"You run across him before?"

"You might say that," Frank replied. "McMasters is the one killed Matt and Luke, then took us in to be hung."

"Only, thanks to Paco here, we didn't hang," Curly said.

"I tol' you Paco was a good man," Michaels said, quickly.

"Yeah, we're all good men," Cantrell said. "But right now I'd like to know more about this McMasters fella."

Cantrell didn't have to wait long to hear about him, for the Dobbs brothers weren't the only ones who knew about Boyd McMasters. Pajarito was just the kind of town that attracted people who had run afoul of Boyd, so there were several who were anxious to tell what they knew about him. Cantrell had never run into McMasters before his attempted train robbery, so he listened atten-
.tively.

"His name is McMasters alright, but I've also sometimes heard him called Bullet," one of the outlaws said.

"Bullet? Why Bullet?" Cantrell asked.

"I don't rightly know, lessen it has somethin' to do with that cannon he shoots. They say the bullets in that thing are the size of a man's fist."

"Bullshit. Nobody could hold onto a gun that would shoot bullets that big."

"They're big bullets," Curly said. "I seen what they done to Matt and Luke."

"Yeah, and I seen what they did to Deermont. Pret' near blowed his arm off," Michaels said. "Hell, you know yourself, Cantrell, Deermont bled to death before we could do anythin' to stop it."

"Deermont was a good man. It ain't right he should'a died like that."

"Matt and Luke was good men, too," Frank said.

"And don't forget Porterfield and Slater," Michaels added.

"Seems to me like it would be doin' ever'one a big favor if someone would just kill that McMasters fella," Cantrell said.

"You goin' to do it?" Curly asked. "Cause if you are, you sure got my blessin'."

"What about your help?"

Curly shook his head. "Don't forget, me an' Frank has tangled with him before. I don't aim to run across him again if I can help it."

"That's just it. We're not goin' to be able to help it," Cantrell replied. "Not if we pull off this job I'm plannin'. But I would be willin' to pay fifty dollars to someone who *would* kill him."

"Ha! Who the hell's goin' to go after Bullet McMasters for fifty dollars?"

"Nobody in their right mind would," Cantrell agreed. "But if I was to come up with fifty, maybe ten more men could come up with fifty also."

"That would be five hundred dollars," someone said.

"That's a lot of money," another suggested.

"Yes, it is. I hope it's enough money to get someone interested in takin' on the job."

There was another man at the table listening to the conversation, but saying nothing. Finally he leaned forward. "Make it six hundred and I might be interested," he said.

"Why six hundred?"

"For six hundred, me an' Spense and Toombs will do the job. That would give us two hundred apiece."

"You think you *could* do it?" Cantrell asked. "You heard what the Dobbses said. Somebody like McMasters takes a lot of killin'."

The man Taggert wore a black hat with a silver band, and he pushed it back on his head.

"Hell," he said. "Me an' Spense and Toombs has *done* a lot of killin'."

"When will you do it?" Cantrell asked.

"Soon as we get the money."

Cantrell shook his head no. "You ain't goin' to get the money till the job is done," he said. "But I'll get the money together and leave it with Moose." Moose Jones and his Mexican wife, Rosita, owned the cantina. "You trust Moose, don't you?"

"Yeah, I trust him."

"All right, you kill McMasters and Moose will give you the money."

"Wait a minute," one of the others intervened. "How will we know if he killed him or not?"

"Hell, that ain't no problem," Curly said. "I can tell you right now, nobody is goin' to *try* and kill Mc-Masters. They either goin' to kill 'im, or they goin' to die. It's as simple as that. If Taggert gets back here alive, then you got to figure that McMasters is dead."

Taggert smiled. "Far as I'm concerned, you can figure he's as good as dead right now," he said.

"Good as, don't mean he's dead," Curly said.

"He will be," Taggert promised.

Crittenden

There were two dozen chairs set up in four rows of six at the bank. The occasion was the official recognition of the bank as a protected member of the Cattleman's Association. In addition, Richard Adams was going to honor the service Captain Boyd McMasters, of the Cattleman's Protective Association, had already performed for the First Territorial Bank of Crittenden.

If Boyd had had his way, there wouldn't have been anything made of it. He would simply validate that the bank had passed his inspection and that would be that. But an exchange of telegrams between Richard Adams, President and owner of the Bank of Crittenden, and Borden McMasters, Vice-President of the Cattleman's Protective Association, made it clear that both the Cattleman's Association, and the Cattleman's Protective Association wanted Boyd to attend the ceremony in good cheer. The fact that the vice-president of the Cattleman's Protective Association was Boyd's brother made Boyd's participation more compelling.

There were to be several guests present for the ceremony. Half a dozen of the county's largest ranchers were there. Angus Waddle was there, as was Sheriff Lindsey and Doc. The other two players of the ongoing poker game were conspicuous by their absense. Pete, who managed, but did not own the livery, was not there because he was not considered a substantial enough depositor. Samantha Chance, who owned the Second Chance Saloon, was a substantial enough depositor, but as being a saloon owner was deemed an unseemly occupation for a woman, she was left off the guest list.

Richard Adams was the host and he greeted Boyd effusively when he arrived.

"Ah, Captain McMasters, good, good, you are here on time I see. I would like to introduce you to some important men."

One by one, Boyd was introduced to the Pima County ranchers. Though one of the ranchers was an Englishman who had bought his spread with old, unearned money, the others were men who had arrived in the territory a long time ago. They were honorable men who had carved their ranches out of the desert, fighting drought, Indians, and outlaws until they were successful. Boyd felt a sense of kinship with them, for there had been a time when he had harbored that same ambition.

"And this is my wife, Millicent," Adams said, taking him over to the table where a young woman of serene beauty stood, dispensing punch.

"It is an honor to meet you, Captain McMasters," Mrs. Adams said. Her voice was softly modulated, with a cultured accent. Boyd was surprised to hear her introduced as Adams's wife. Had he been asked to make a guess, he would have suggested that this was his daughter, for she was in her twenties, while Adams was clearly in his late fifties.

Adams made a short speech, acknowledging his bank's acceptance for protection by the Cattleman's Protective Association. Then he handed Boyd a letter of commendation for his performance against the would-be train robbers, informing Boyd that this was but a copy of the letter that had been sent to the vice-president of the company itself.

"And now, if you would please, I would like to show all of you our new vault," Adams invited when the speech was over. "We are quite proud of the vault, aren't we, Mr. Beckworth?"

Beckworth was the chief teller.

"Oh, indeed we are, sir," Beckworth said. He was wearing a gray jacket and striped trousers, a high-wing collar shirt and a bow tie. His pince-nez glasses set on the end of his nose, and though at first glance they seemed precariously perched, Boyd saw that Beckworth was actually quite comfortable with them.

Boyd had already seen the vault when he inspected the bank. However, as he deemed this to be a part of the ceremony that his brother had asked him to attend, he followed the others through the tour, viewing the safe yet again.

"It is called an American Standard," Beckworth explained, standing proudly in front of the big safe. The heavy door was painted light green, while the trim and lettering were in a darker shade. "The door is four-inch-thick steel, and it is locked by four steel bars, each two inches in diameter. In addition, the tumblers are absolutely silent so that no one can pick the lock."

"What if someone blasted it open?" one of the ranchers asked.

"If someone attempted to blast the vault open with dynamite, they would destroy the building before they opened the safe."

"It sounds pretty secure, all right," one of the cattlemen said.

"It has to be secure," Adams replied. "As of this morning we have on deposit . . . how much, Beckworth?"

"Fifty-eight thousand, six hundred and fourteen dollars, and thirty-two cents," Beckworth said with the easy familiarity of someone who worked daily with other people's money.

"For my money, one member of the Cattleman's Protective Association like Boyd McMasters is worth half a dozen of those safes," one of the other ranchers said.

"Here, here," the others replied, and several applauded politely.

Boyd accepted their accolades self-consciously, then, when the others found another part of the bank to explore, he walked back out front, detaching himself from the group. Seeing him alone, Millie Adams came over to bring him a cup of punch.

"Thanks," Boyd said without real enthusiasm. He took a swallow, then noticed that it was actually quite heavily spiked. He looked at Millie in surprise and gratitude, and she smiled.

"I thought you looked as if you might need it," she said. "You aren't very comfortable in these type of situations, are you?"

"No," Boyd admitted. "I don't know why your husband went to all the trouble to do this. All I really had to do was sign a certificate and the bank would be covered.''

Millie laughed, a light, lyrical laugh. "Captain McMasters, don't you understand? My husband isn't doing this for you or for the Association. He's doing this for his own personal business reasons. Within a week the newspapers in Phoenix, Tucson, Tombstone, perhaps even Denver, will carry this story, and it will give Richard yet another opportunity to show how safe the bank is. And he will be able to solicit more depositors.''

"I guess I didn't think about that.''

"That's all right. Most people don't think the way Richard does. I suppose I'm a good example of the way his mind works.''

"You?''

Millie laughed again. "Surely, Captain, it hasn't escaped your notice that there is quite a difference between my husband's age and my own.''

"Oh, uh, yes.''

"Don't you wonder why he would marry someone like me?''

Boyd smiled. "You are a beautiful and charming woman, Mrs. Adams. What is there to wonder?''

"You are too kind. Actually, Richard married me for the same reason he does everything else. He married me because it was good for his business. My father, you see, owns a substantial shipping line in Baltimore. By marrying me, Richard has a connection to old Eastern money. He doesn't actually have the money, you understand . . . my father is very conservative and isn't about to commit any funds to a small bank way out here in the Arizona Territory. But I dare say Richard has realized some business advantages through the connection, nevertheless.''

"That explains why he married you. Why did you marry him?''

A shadow crossed her eyes for a moment, then, with cool control, she put the shadow aside, smiling once again.

"Let us just say that I had my reasons,'' she replied.

"I'm sorry. I had no right to pry.''

"No need to apologize, Captain. I brought it up myself. I fear, however, that I have been a bit too loquacious. And now, if you will excuse me, I should see to my daughter. She is in the other room, out of the way. She is quite good at entertaining herself, but I do need to check on her. Would you like to meet her?''

"Yes, I would.''

Boyd followed Millie into another room just off the main part of the bank. A little girl of about five was sitting at a table, drawing pictures.

"Look, Mother,'' the little girl said, speaking in a voice that was already almost as cultured as that of Mrs. Adams. "I have drawn a tree. It is quite a lovely tree, don't you think?''

"Oh, yes, very lovely,'' Millie said. "Linda, this is Captain McMasters.''

Linda got up from her chair and walked over to extend her hand.

"I am pleased to meet you, Captain McMasters,'' she said. "You are the one who saved the money for Papa's bank, aren't you?''

"Yes,'' Boyd replied.

"Then you may have this tree,'' Linda said, offering the drawing.

"Oh, no, I couldn't take it."

"Oh yes, please do. I can always draw another one, can't I, Mother?"

"Yes," Millie said, smiling at her daughter. "You can always draw another one."

The drawing was on the table beside him when Boyd ate his dinner that evening. He was eating in the dining room and though Sam was there as well, he didn't offer to sit at her table, knowing how fiercely Sam protected her independence. She finished her own dinner, then came over to speak to Boyd as she was leaving.

"Will you be playing cards again tonight?" she asked.

"As long as I'm winning more than I'm losing, I'll continue to play," Boyd replied.

"Good, I'll see you there, then. Oh, what's this?" she asked, seeing the drawing.

"That is a tree," Boyd explained. "The little Adams girl drew it."

"Linda?"

"Yes, I think that is her name. Have you ever talked to her? She doesn't talk much like a little girl."

"Yes, I know. She has an amazing vocabulary," Sam said. She examined the picture for a long moment. There was a strange, almost longing look in her eyes. "Boyd, may I have this?" she asked in a quiet voice.

"Sure, if you really want it."

"I really want it."

"Then take it," Boyd said easily. "It's yours."

"Thank you." Sam blinked a couple of times and

Boyd almost thought he saw tears in her eyes. He realized then that she probably really would like to have children of her own. Boyd could understand that. Hannah had wanted children.

Six

Taggert, Spense, and Toombs rode into Crittenden just after dark. The street was dimly illuminated by squares of yellow light which spilled through the doors and windows of the buildings. High above the little town, stars winked brightly, while over a distant mesa the moon hung like a large silver wheel.

"What do you say we get a drink?" Taggert suggested.

"Hell, Taggert, you ain't goin' to get any argument from us on that," Spense answered.

The three men tied off their horses then went into the Second Chance Saloon. The barkeep slid down the bar toward them.

"What can I get you gents?"

"Whiskey," Taggert said. "Leave the bottle."

"What kind?"

"The cheapest. We want to get drunk, not give a party."

The bartender took a bottle from beneath the counter. There was no label on the bottle and the color of the alcohol was dingy. He put three glasses alongside the bottle, then pulled the cork for them.

"There it is," he said.

Taggert poured a glass, then passed it down. He took a swallow, then almost gagged. He spit it out and frowned at his glass.

"Goddamn!" he said. "This tastes like horse piss."

Spense took a smaller swallow. He grimaced, but he got it down. Toombs had no problem with it at all.

"It's all in the way you drink it," Toombs explained. "This here whiskey can't be drunk down real fast. You got to sort of sip it."

Taggert tried again, and this time he, too, managed to keep it down.

There was an animated conversation going on at the other end of the bar:

"If you think the hole in his chest was somethin', you should'a seen the hole in his back. When it was comin' out, that bullet blowed half his spine away," someone was saying.

"Yeah, and the other one, did you see his neck? I tell you the truth, it's a wonder that gun didn't blow his head clean off."

"Iffen ol' Slater had been a mite thinner, it would've blowed his head off."

"Yeah, well, if you'd'a seen the size of the gun McMasters was carryin', you wouldn't be surprised by the damage it done."

"Hey, Taggert," Spense whispered. "You hear what they're talkin' about?"

"Yeah," Taggert replied. He moved down the bar toward the three men who were involved in the conversation. " 'Scuse me, gents, but me an' my two pards been on the trail for so long we ain't heard no news 'bout nothin'. Mind if we listen in on your palaver?"

"We're talkin' 'bout the train robbery the other night," one of the men said.

"Only they didn't get nothin' on account of what happened," one of the others clarified.

"What happened?"

"It just so happened that Bullet McMasters was on the train when the robbers hit it. I 'spect you may have heard of him. He's a captain in the Cattleman's Protective Association? Anyhow, McMasters clumb up on top of that rail car and commenced bangin' away at the robbers with that gun of his'n."

"And that there's the gun we was talkin' about. Bullet McMasters got it bored out for a .70-caliber, you see. And it blowed holes in them two robbers he kilt like as if he was shootin' cannonballs."

"They say he kilt three of 'em. There was one more he hit that got away into the desert. Like as not he's dead by now, too."

"I guess this here Bullet fella is quite a hero around here now," Taggert said.

"I'll say he is. They even give him a reward at the bank today."

"Ha! Some reward. All he got was a letter sayin' how thankful the bank was that he saved the money for 'em. They didn't give him no kind of money reward at all."

"I don't think he can take money. I mean, him bein' a captain in the Cattleman's Protective Association and all. That's pret' near like bein' a sheriff or something, isn't it? I don't think he can take money."

"He don't need to take no money, the kind of luck he's been havin' at cards. He's back there right now, prob'ly winnin' tonight like he's been winnin' ever' night since he come here."

"You say he's back there playin' cards right now?" Taggert said.

"Sure is. You can't miss him. He's the dark-haired fella with the blue shirt."

While the others continued to talk, Taggert poured himself another drink, then walked to the back of the saloon to look around into the little alcove where the card game was being played. Taggert stood there, sipping his drink for a while, studying this man they called Bullet McMasters.

"Bullet," he said under his breath. "You don't look all that tough to me."

The cards weren't running that well for Boyd tonight. By hedging his bets and by maximizing his good hands and minimizing his bad, he managed to stay a little ahead, but the big winner tonight was Sam.

When the game was over, Boyd told the others goodnight, then went next door to the hotel and up to his room. He lit the lantern and walked over to the window to adjust it to catch the night breeze. That was when he saw a sudden flash of light in the hayloft over the livery across the street. He knew he was seeing a muzzle flash even before he heard the gun report, and he was already pulling away from the window at the precise instant a bullet crashed through the glass of the window and slammed into the wall on the opposite side of the room.

Someone was shooting at him! He cursed himself for the foolish way he had exposed himself at the window. He was a professional, and as a professional he knew better.

There were two other shots on the heels of the first, so close together that Boyd knew there had to be three men. The only thing he could think of was the Dobbs brothers. Had they gotten help and come after him?

Boyd reached up to extinguish the lantern, then he grabbed his rifle and jacked a round into the chamber.

"What was that?" someone shouted from down on the street.

"Gunshots. Sounded like they came from the . . ."

That was as far as the disembodied voice got before another volley of three shots crashed through the window. If Boyd thought the first volley had cleaned out all the glass he was mistaken, for there was another shattering tinkling sound of bullets crashing through glass.

"Get off the street!" Boyd heard a voice, loud and authoritative, floating up from below. "Everyone, get inside!"

Boyd recognized the voice. It belonged to Harley Gibbons, Sheriff Lindsey's deputy.

"Harley, stay away!" Boyd shouted. He raised up to look through the window and saw Harley heading for the livery stable with his pistol in his hand. "Harley, no! Get back!"

Boyd's warning was too late. A third volley was fired from the livery hayloft, and Harley fell facedown in the street.

This time, however, Boyd was ready for them, and he aimed just to the right of where the flame pattern had appeared. That meant he would be shooting through a one-inch-thick board, for the shooters in the loft were using the walls as cover, just peeking around the edge of the loft door, whenever they wanted to take a shot.

Boyd's gun boomed, a deep, heavy-throated roar which rolled up and down the street. The bullet crashed through the livery wall, then a body tumbled through the open loft door, hitting hard and raising dust where it fell onto the street below.

"Son of a bitch! a voice shouted from within the livery. "He shot Toombs right through the wall!"

Who was Toombs? Boyd didn't know anyone named Toombs.

Boyd fired again, but this time it was just to keep the shooters' heads down, for he knew that, by now, they would have figured out that they weren't safe from his big gun just because they were behind a wall.

Taking advantage of their looking for more secure cover, Boyd left the rifle behind him, took one of his pistols, then climbed out of the window, scrambled to the edge of the porch and dropped down onto the street. He ran to Harley's still form, then bent down to check the deputy out. Harley was clearly dead.

"There he is, Spense!" a voice shouted. "He's down there by the deputy!" Two more rifle shots were fired. The bullets hit the ground close by, then ricochetted away with a loud whine. Boyd fired back, shooting twice into the dark maw of the hayloft. He ran to the water trough nearest the livery and dove behind it as the outlaws fired again. Both bullets hit the trough with a loud *thock*.

He had heard two names now. Toombs and Spense. He didn't recognize either name. Perhaps this wasn't the Dobbs brothers.

Boyd could hear the water gurgling through the bullet holes in the water trough as he got up and ran toward the door of the livery. He shot two more times to keep the assailants back. When he reached the big, open double doors of the livery, he ran on through so that he was inside.

"Where'd he go? Taggert, do you see him?"

"I think he come inside."

Taggert, Toombs, and Spense. Now he knew the names, but he didn't know the men, and he didn't know why they were trying to kill him.

"Taggert!" the voice called again. "Do you see him?"

"No," Taggert answered.

Boyd moved quietly through the barn itself, looking up at the hayloft just overhead. Suddenly he felt little pieces of hay falling on him and he stopped, because he realized that someone had to be right over him. Then he heard it, a quiet shuffling of feet. Boyd fired twice, straight up, then he heard a groan and a loud thump.

"That's six shots. You're out of bullets, you son of a bitch," a calm voice said. Boyd looked over to his left to see a man standing openly on the edge of the loft. The man was holding a rifle and, inexplicably, he laughed. "I ought to thank you for killin' Spense and Toombs like you done. That just leaves more money for me." He raised his rifle to his shoulder, and Boyd fired.

"What?" the outlaw gasped in shock, dropping his rifle and clutching the wound in his stomach.

"Surprise, Taggert. This one shoots seven," Boyd said flatly. He watched as the man fell from the loft, flipping over so as to land on his back in the dirt below. Boyd walked over to look down at him.

"McMasters! McMasters, are you all right?" It was the sheriff's voice.

"I'm in here, Sheriff," he said.

Lindsey came running in then, puffing from the exertion. He was holding his pistol and he looked down at the body.

"Poor Harley's dead," Lindsey said.

"Yeah, I know."

"Were there two of them? I saw one lying out front."

"Three," Boyd replied. "The one out front, this one, and one up in the loft."

"You know 'em?"

"I heard their names called out," Boyd said. "Taggert, Spense, and Toombs. Mean anything to you?"

"I think I've got paper on them. They normally hang out over around Pajarito. Don't know what they were doin' over here, though. What were they after, do you know?"

"They were after me."

"You?"

Boyd sighed. "This one said that by killing Spense and Toombs, I had fixed it so he would get more money. I believe the outlaws must have some paper out on me." He chuckled. "I wonder how much I'm worth."

Cantrell, Michaels, Curly, Frank, and Paco rode toward Crittenden the next morning. Cantrell explained that he planned to leave Curly, Frank, and Paco camped out in a ravine in the shadow of the Sierrita Mountains, while he and Michaels rode on into town.

"No sense in all of us ridin' into town at one time," Cantrell explained. "If they's just the two of us, folks will take no mind. But five of us might cause some folks to start wonderin'."

"You just make sure you come back here 'fore you go after the money," Frank said.

" 'Course we're comin' back," Cantrell said. "Hell, if we could'a done it alone, I wouldn' ask you to come along in the first place."

"Yeah," Frank said. "Yeah, I guess that's right, ain't it? Okay, we'll wait here."

Crittenden was quiet when the two rode in. It was nearly noon and many of the Mexicans were taking their siesta, though some sat or stood in the shade of the porch over-hangs. A game of checkers was being played by two old men, one American and one Mexican, in front of the feedstore. Half a dozen onlookers were following the game intently. One or two looked up as Cantrell and Michaels rode by, their horses' hooves clumping hol-lowly on the hard-packed earth of the street.

A shopkeeper came through the front door of his shop and began sweeping vigorously with a straw broom. The broom raised a lot of dust and pushed a sleeping dog off the porch, but even before the man went back inside, the dog reclaimed its position in the shade, curled com-fortably around itself, and was asleep again.

"Hey, Cantrell," Michaels said. "Take a look up there."

Michaels was pointing to the front of the hardware store where a handful of people had gathered around to stare at three coffins which were standing on end. The pine coffins, narrow at the top, flaring out for the shoul-ders, then tapering back to a narrow bottom, were all occupied.

All three corpses had their arms folded across their chests. All three had their eyes open, looking ahead with the opaque stare of death.

"Wonder where Taggert's hat is?" Michaels asked matter-of-factly. "Wouldn't mind havin' that silver band for my ownself."

"Undertaker prob'ly stole it," Cantrell said.

"Son of a bitch. Can't trust anyone these days," Michaels said.

The two men nudged their horses on.

"Let's go in here an' get somethin' to drink," Cantrell suggested. "And maybe a little somethin' to eat."

The talk in the saloon was about the gun battle that had taken place the night before. Cantrell and Michaels monitored the disjointed conversation as they ate their meal. Neither of them had ever been in Crittenden before, so they didn't know anyone who was speaking. Therefore, they made no effort to connect the statements with individual speakers. They just listened to the whole, absorbing the information:

"How come they don't have Harley's body out there with the others? It don't seem right to me."

"Why should he be out there with the others? He was a good man, those men were outlaws."

"That's what I'm talkin' about. Here them outlaws is made out to be heroes while poor ol' Harley is lyin' over there in the funeral parlor without anyone payin' any attention to him a'tall. 'Cept his wife."

"That ain't true. His friends has all been to see him. And Ponder took pains to dress ol' Harley in his new suit and fix him up so's he looks just real natural. You seen them outlaws ain't you? Ponder didn't do nothin' for them but embalm 'em. And, don't forget, Mr. Adams also give Harley's widder a hundred dollars. He says he believes them three come here to rob the bank and Harley and McMasters stopped 'em."

"Rob the bank? What makes him think they was goin' to rob the bank? They weren't nowhere near the bank. Besides that, it was at night.''

''Mr. Adams thinks they was tryin' to kill off the law first. Then they was goin' to go down there and hold up the bank. That's why he's hired him a couple of full-time guards to watch over it.''

''I feel sorry for anyone who's fool enough to try an' rob this bank now. In the first place, they ain't no way anyone can get that safe open 'less they know the combination. And in the second place they's now a couple of full-time guards workin' down there every moment the bank is open.''

''Plus, don't forget that whoever tries anything is goin' to have to deal with the Cattleman's Protective Association. I mean, even if they was to kill Bullet McMasters, there's a whole bunch more out there to take his place.''

''Yeah, well let me tell you somethin'. My money's in that bank an' if I hear someone's tryin' to get it, they goin' to have me to deal with.''

''One of the others laughed. ''You goin' up against the bank robbers?''

''Didn't say I was goin' to face 'em down. I just said they'd have me to deal with. Iffen I see someone in that bank that don't belong, I'm goin' to hide somewhere along the street with a loaded, ten-gauge Greener. When the robbers come out, I'll give 'em a belly full of double-aught buckshot.''

''You wouldn't be alone. I got money in there, too.''

''By God, we all do. I reckon we could give 'em a reception, all right! There's been more'n one bank robber shot down by ordinary citizens.''

''Hey, maybe we should all go see Mr. Adams an'

see if he'd hire us as guards," someone joked, and the others laughed.

"Yeah. We could just all go down to the end of the street to that big white house of his and ask if he'd take us on."

"Are you kiddin'? Adams is so cheap he's got that big house down there and he ain't got servant one to help run it. That little ol' girl he's got for a wife has to take care of the whole thing, all by herself."

"That's somethin' ain't it? I bet there ain't a house no nicer, or bigger this side of Denver. But for all the rooms he's got, they don't no one live in it but Adams, his wife, and that little girl of their'n."

"How'd somebody as old an' ugly as Adams get him such a young, good-lookin' wife?"

"If a man is rich enough, I guess he can afford to have a young, pretty woman for a wife."

"What good does it do him to be rich if he don't use his money to make things any easier? I mean, there she is, married to the richest man in town, but she works harder than the commonest *señora* over in Mex Town. I tell you what, If I had a young, pretty wife like that, and I had the money to afford it, I sure wouldn't make her work like a slave."

"You been hearin' all that?" Cantrell asked, quietly.

"Can't much help it," Michaels replied. "That's all they been talkin' about. I tell you what, Cantrell, it don't sound to me like that bank's goin' to be all that easy to get into."

"Yeah," Cantrell said. "Maybe we'll have to come up with another plan."

"What other plan?" Michaels asked. "The money's

in the bank. If we're goin' to get it, that's where we're goin' to have to go."

"Let me think about it," Cantrell replied. "We've come this far, I don't aim to let that money get away from us."

Seven

"It'll never work," Curly said when Cantrell explained his plan to the others. "I say we just ride in this afternoon, hit the bank before they know what's goin' on, grab the money, and leave."

"Yeah, I'm with Curly," Frank said.

"Didn't you fellas listen to what I said?" Cantrell asked. "I told you, they got two armed guards there all day long. And all that clerk has to do, if he gets wind of what we're doin', is slam the vault door shut and there ain't nothin' we can do about it."

"All right, but I don't like it that just two of you are goin' in," Frank said. "That means you will have all the money."

"Which will be split up as soon as we get back," Cantrell said.

"How do we know you'll come back?"

"We have to come back. McMasters will be on our trail like stink on shit. But he'll only know about the two of us. When he comes after us, you will be waiting. You kill him . . . that's how you earn your cut."

"We get our cut before we set up the ambush?" Frank asked.

"Yes."

Frank stroked his chin. "What do you think, Curly?" he asked his brother.

"I don't see no problem with it," Curly replied. "Besides, I been waitin' to get even with that son of a bitch ever since he killed Matt an' Luke."

"What about you, Paco? You afraid he'll cheat us out of our cut?" Frank asked.

"I do not think he will cheat us," Paco replied. He was cleaning his fingernails with his knife. "If he does, I do not think he will ever cheat anyone again." He emphasized his statement by a pantomime of pulling his knife across his throat.

"Yeah," Frank said. He looked at Cantrell. "You'd better pay attention to that, too, 'cause I'm tellin' you for a fact that Paco knows how to use that knife. All right, you two go into town for the money. We'll wait out here."

"After we make the cut, you take care of Mc-Masters," Cantrell said.

"We'll do our part, you just do yours," Frank growled.

The night creatures called to each other as Cantrell and Michaels sat astride their horses just outside Crittenden. A cloud passed over the moon, then moved away, bathing in silver the little town that rose up like a ghost before them. The largest building in town, larger even than the hotel, was a big white house that stood at the end of the street with its cupolas, dormers, balconies, porches, and gingerbread trim, all shining brightly in the moonlight. The property was surrounded by a white picket fence, which enclosed not only the house, but a carriage house and stable as well.

"Let's go," Cantrell said. "We'll tie the horses off in the stable at the back of the property. That way no one will notice a couple of strange horses hangin' around the house."

The two men rode slowly into town, avoiding the main street and approaching from an angle that would be least likely to be noticed. When they reached the stable behind the big white house, they dismounted, then tied their horses off just inside the carriage house. One of the stabled horses snorted, as if questioning these un-invited guests, but the interrogation died with one whicker.

From the shadows of the stable the two men moved out into the bright moonlight, picking their way carefully and quietly across the backyard. The back door to the house was locked, but Cantrell stuck his knife in be-tween the door edge and the lock plate and had it open in a couple of seconds.

They slipped inside. This was the kitchen and the big cookstove loomed over one side of the room, giving off a faint aroma of the pork it had cooked for supper. There was a white cloth at one end, and as they walked by Michaels lifted the cloth. Under the cloth was a plate with a couple of cold pork chops, and half a pan of biscuits.

"Hey, Cantrell, look," Michaels whispered.

"Leave it alone."

"The hell you say."

Michaels grabbed a pork chop, pulled the meat away from the bone, then stuck it into a biscuit. He dropped the bone on the floor. Then, eating his impromptu sup-per, he followed Cantrell through the rest of the house.

A spill of moonlight illuminated the parlor and showed, clearly, the bottom of the stairs. They started up the stairs and were on the third step when there was a sudden whirring sound, followed by two *bongs*. It was the clock, striking two A.M.

"Son-of-a-bitch," Michaels whispered. "That scared the bejesus out of me."

"Keep quiet," Cantrell warned.

They continued to the top of the stairs. Slowly, quietly, they moved to the nearest bedroom, then opened the door. The same splash of moonlight that had illuminated the parlor also illuminated this room and they could see a woman, sleeping alone.

"What the hell? Where's Adams?" Michaels asked, surprised to see the woman alone.

Michaels started on down the hall.

"Where you goin'?" Cantrell asked.

"To look for Adams," Michaels answered.

"Don't need to," Cantrell replied. "The woman here is all we need."

Quietly, Cantrell and Michaels moved on into the room, then stood over the woman's bed, looking down at her. She was wearing a silk sleeping gown and, because it was very warm, she was sleeping on top of the covers. Even in the moonlight, Cantrell could see her nipples pushing against the silk and he felt a sudden, powerful erection. For a moment he was ready to forget what he was here for, but he managed to put the urge down. He pulled his pistol from his holster, then he bent down and clamped his hand over her mouth.

The woman awoke with a start, and, looking up to see Cantrell staring down at her, tried to scream, only to have it cut off by increased pressure from Cantrell's hand.

"You just lie there real quiet-like and you won't get hurt," Cantrell hissed in the darkness.

The woman's eyes were opened wide in terror.

"Where at's your husband?"

She continued to stare at him with fear-crazed eyes.

"He in the house?"

The woman made no attempt to answer, and Cantrell cocked his pistol.

"Shake your head yes or no, lady," Cantrell said gruffly. "Is he in the house?"

The woman shook her head yes.

"I'm goin' to take my hand away now," Cantrell said. "You make a sound, I'm goin' to blow your brains out. Then I'm goin' to kill your husband and your kid." Slowly, he pulled his hand away.

"What . . . what do you want?" the woman asked in a small, frightened voice.

"I want you to lead me into your husband's room. Then I want you to wake him up."

The woman nodded, then got out of bed. Seeing the clinging silk gown made Cantrell's erection grow stronger, and he was having a difficult time concentrating on what he was doing.

"He's in there," she said.

"Let's go."

Cantrell and Michaels followed her out of her room, across the hall, and into the bedroom of her husband. He was snoring.

"Wake him up."

"Richard? Richard?" the woman called.

The snoring halted for a moment, then continued.

"I said wake him up, lady."

"Richard!"

Adams snorted and wheezed. "What?" he asked. "What is it? What do you want? I told you earlier tonight, I'm not in the mood to . . ."

"Richard, there are some men here."

"What?"

"I said there are some men here," the woman said, her voice breaking with fear.

"What do you mean, men?" Adams asked. He reached for the bedside lantern, lit it, then turned it up so that the room was bathed in light. Then he picked up his glasses and put them on, fitting them very carefully over one ear at a time. That was when he saw the two men standing by his wife. "My God!" he gasped, jumping up quickly. "What is this?"

"This here is a bank robbery, Mr. Adams," Cantrell said easily.

"What do you mean a bank robbery? Are you crazy? I don't keep any money in my house."

"I know you don't. But you are the banker. And this here is your wife." Cantrell pointed the gun toward the woman's head, putting the barrel against her temple. "Now what I want you to do is, go down there to your bank, get out that there fifty thousand dollars I hear that you got, and bring it back to me."

"Why on earth would I want to do a damn fool thing like that?"

"Because if you don't do it, I'm going to kill your wife and your kid right here in front of you," Cantrell growled. "And then I am going to kill you."

"I'm . . . I'm not at all sure I can even do what you are asking," Adams stammered. "The money is in a vault. It has a difficult lock. I don't normally open it. My chief teller is in charge of that."

"You'd better figure out how to do it," Cantrell said easily. " 'Cause if you ain't back in half an hour, we kill the woman and the kid."

"Richard, for heavens' sake, do what they ask," the woman said.

"Just be calm, Millie," Adams said. "I don't believe they really mean you any harm."

"Tell you what," Cantrell said. "Just to show you we're serious, if you ain't back in twenty minutes, me an' my friend here are goin' to start havin' a little fun with your wife, if you know what I mean." He rubbed himself, pointedly. "Then, after we've had our fun with her, if you still ain't back with the money, we're goin' to kill her."

"All right, all right," Adams said, holding his hands out toward them. "I'll get dressed. I'll get the money."

Quickly, Adams pulled on his trousers and a shirt, then he slipped on his shoes. Finally he was ready to go.

"Remember, twenty minutes," Cantrell said. "Be back here in twenty minutes with the money, or the fun starts." He reached over to grab one of Millie's breasts, squeezing it hard enough for her to gasp with pain.

"It is not necessary for you to do that."

Cantrell smiled evilly. "Well, now, that's all up to you, ain't it? Want me to tell you the truth? I hope you don't make it back before the twenty minutes is up."

After Adams left, Cantrell looked over at Millie. Her eyes reflected her terror, but she was fighting hard to keep herself under control.

"What a cool bitch you are," Cantrell said.

"Would it do me any good to scream?" Millie asked.

Cantrell chuckled. "No," he said. "None at all. Sit in that chair."

Millie did as he directed, sitting in a straight-back wooden chair.

"Michaels, tie her hands behind the chair."

"That won't be necessary," Millie said. "I won't give you any trouble."

"You're damn right you won't," Cantrell said. He tossed a short piece of rope to Michaels. "Do what I said."

Michaels pulled Millie's arms around behind the chair, then tied her hands. As he did so, it made her breasts push into the silk nightgown, both nipples clearly visible in relief.

"Yeah," Cantrell said, nodding in appreciation. "Oh, yeah, you look fine."

"Let me see," Michaels said, moving around front of the chair to stare.

Millie's face burned in shame, but she said nothing.

Cantrell took out his knife, then started toward her.

"You ain't goin' to cut her, are you, Cantrell?"

Millie closed her eyes and took a deep breath. She felt the point of the knife sticking her through the nightgown, just between the breasts. She felt his hand move quickly and she gasped in fear, then relief as she felt, not the sting of the blade, but the coolness of the night air. Cantrell had just cut her nightgown.

"Let's get a better look," Cantrell said, and he took the two halves of the nightgown then split it all the way down. He pulled it down across her shoulders so that her frontal nudity was completely exposed to their lustful staring.

"You are one fine-lookin' woman, lady," Cantrell said, speaking in a voice that was almost respectful. "You could go 'on the line' and make yourself a rich woman, did you know that? Yes, ma'am, there's just lots of people would pay dear to get into your drawers."

"Her tits is too little," Michaels complained. "I like women with big tits."

"You been hangin' around them melon-tittied Mexican whores too much," Cantrell said.

"I like whores with melon-sized tits," Michaels insisted. Michaels walked over and looked out the window. "Here he is, comin' back," he said.

"Is he carrying anything?"

"He's carryin' a big sack."

Cantrell smiled broadly. "That's our money!" he said. "Son of a bitch, Michaels! We done it! We took this bank!"

Adams came into the house, then up the stairs.

"I got the money," he said.

"How much did you get?"

"I got every cent that was in the bank. Fifty eight thousand dollars." He looked over toward the chair and saw Millie sitting there, her nightgown torn in two. "What have you done to her?"

"We ain't done nothin' to her," Cantrell said, opening the sack and pulling out several stacks of bills. "Go ahead, untie her if you want." Adams untied Millie's hands, and she brought them around in front of her, rubbing them gingerly.

"For God's sake, Millicent, cover yourself," Adams said.

Millie pulled the nightgown back together, then

clutched it with one hand. She stood up and started toward Richard.

"No!" he said. "My God, woman, do you think I could touch you now? After this?"

"After what?" Millie asked innocently.

"After you have been . . . defiled in this way."

"They didn't hurt me."

"I daresay they didn't. You probably enjoyed it, wanton hussy that you are. I haven't forgotten the circumstance under which you left Baltimore. Seems to me like I'm the one who has been defiled here and I won't stand for it. By God I won't stand for it."

Richard moved quickly, running out into the landing toward the hall tree. He jerked open the drawer and reached inside.

"Hey, what the hell?" Cantrell shouted in surprise when he saw Richard run out of the room. Cantrell dropped the money bag and pulled his pistol. "What are you doin'? Get back in here!" he shouted.

"I'll not be disgraced in this way!" Adams shouted. He was fumbling around inside the hall tree drawer.

"Get out of that drawer!" Cantrell shouted, pointing his pistol at Adams.

Adams pulled a short-barreled pistol out of the drawer and swung it toward Cantrell. Cantrell pulled the trigger, the gun boomed in his hand, and the bullet hit Adams square in the middle of the forehead. The banker went down on his back, his arms flopping out to either side, his eyes open and opaque. He was dead before he hit the floor.

Outside, a dog began to bark.

"You dumb bastard!" Cantrell said angrily. He walked over to look down at Adams. He picked up the pistol and put it back in the drawer, then closed it. "What did you make me kill you for? We could've tied you up and left you here. We would've been gone long before anyone discovered you. But you, you stupid son of a bitch! You had to be a hero!"

"What are we going to do now?" Michaels asked.

"I don't know. Let me think," Cantrell said.

The dog continued to bark.

"If someone heard the shot and that dog, they might wonder what's goin' on," Michaels suggested.

"Shut up! Let me think!" Cantrell said. He looked over at the woman. She was standing there, still half nude, looking down in shock at her husband's body.

"Mother! Mother, what was that noise?" a little girl called.

"Shit, the little girl's woke up," Michaels said.

"You!" Cantrell said, pointing to Millie. "Get something on you can ride a horse in. And keep the kid quiet. Make certain she understands that if she ain't quiet I'm goin' to kill you both."

"She is a very intelligent child," Millie said. "She will understand."

"And hurry it up! If you ain't ready to go in five minutes I'll kill you both! Michaels, go down to the stable and saddle one of their horses, then rig a line so we can lead it."

Millie went into the little girl's room and explained in harsh whispers, not only what happened, but what lay in store for them if they weren't quiet, and if they didn't do exactly as they were directed.

"I will be good, Mother," Linda said in a quiet little voice.

Millie had them both dressed in less than five minutes.

Cantrell hurried them down the stairs, herding them as if they were a couple of animals. When they got outside, Michaels had the three horses ready and waiting for them.

"Hurry, hurry!" Cantrell urged.

Going through the gate, Millie caught her dress on the latch. When she jerked, a piece of it tore. She had just had this riding habit made and she felt a sense of frustration over damaging it so quickly. Then, the ludicrousness of being concerned over a torn dress when her very life was in danger struck her as being funny, and she laughed.

"What the hell you laughin' at?" Cantrell asked.

"Nothing," Millie said. "Nothing at all."

"You're crazy," Cantrell said. "I'd be better off killin' you and leavin' you here."

"I'm sorry," Millie said.

"Get mounted," Cantrell growled.

Millie mounted and, because the riding habit was designed to split in the middle, she was able to sit astride the horse. Using the same piece of rope that had been used to tie her hands in the bedroom, he tied her hands to the saddle pommel.

"Are you going to put me on the horse with Mother?" Linda asked.

"You? No, little lady. You're going to ride with Michaels," Cantrell said.

"Hey, not me. I don't want her," Michaels protested.

"You ain't got no choice," Cantrell said, picking the little girl up and putting her on the saddle in front of Michaels. He then mounted and took the line from Millie's horse. He looked back up at the house.

"That dumb son of a bitch. Just look at what he

caused." He clucked at his horse. "Come on," he said. "Let's go."

They rode through the rest of the night. Then, just as the sun was a bright red disc balanced on the eastern horizon, they reached an arroyo. Cantrell held up his arm for them to stop.

"Curly?" he called. "Frank? Paco? Are you fellas here?"

"We're over here," a voice replied from behind a large mesquite tree.

"Did you get the money?" another voice asked.

"Every penny of it," Cantrell replied, holding up the bag.

"Yahoo! Did you hear that, boys? We got the money!" one of the unseen voices said. Millie saw three men come out from behind the mesquite, laughing and shouting, and pounding one another on the back.

"I told you I'd come back," Cantrell said.

"Hey, wait a minute! Who's this?" Curly asked, seeing Millie and Linda. "What the hell are you doin' with them?"

"We had a little problem," Cantrell said.

"What kind of problem?"

"We had to kill the banker. This is his wife an' kid. We took them along as insurance."

"Insurance? Hell, we don't need no insurance. You should'a left them."

"We couldn't leave them. They could identify us."

"And now they've seen us, you dumb son of a bitch," Cruly growled. "You should've killed 'em."

"Don't tell me what I should've done. I've done all right so far. I got the money, didn't I?"

"He's right, Curly," Michaels said. "We got the money."

"Yeah, what's your problem, Curly? We got the money," Frank said. He stared at Millie for a long moment, stroking his chin as he did so. "Yeah," he said again. "We got the money, and we got the woman. So I figure we may as well make the best of it." He started toward Millie, and she cringed back in fear.

"What are you doin'?" Cantrell asked.

"What the hell does it look like I'm doin'? I'm 'bout to have me a little fun."

"You ain't touchin' her," Cantrell said.

"Who the hell says I ain't?" Frank replied.

"I say you ain't," Cantrell said. "Not yet, anyway," he added. "We don't have time for that."

"What do you mean we don't have time? How the hell long do you think it takes to fuck? Three minutes? Four?"

"Cantrell's right, Frank," Curly said. "We got better things to do now. Like get our money." He looked at Cantrell. "How much did we get?"

Cantrell smiled broadly. "We got fifty thousand dollars," he said, conveniently forgetting the extra eight thousand. He reached down into the bag and started pulling out packets of bills. "There's two thousand dollars in each one of these here packets. Your share comes to ten thousand dollars, that's five packets apiece." He started tossing them out one at a time and the tension that had developed over the woman disappeared. Now the men, including Curly, were laughing and shouting as they caught the money packets and stuffed them into their pockets and their shirts.

"Now, tell me, Frank, ain't havin' the banker's

money better'n havin' the banker's wife?" Curly asked.

"Yeah, you're right, who needs her?" Frank replied, mollified now. "With all this money I can go down into Mexico and buy me the best-lookin' whore I can find. No, no, make that the two best-lookin' whores I can find. One for the daytime and one for the night. Then I'm goin' to buy a house and stock it with steak and whiskey and I ain't goin' to do nothin' but eat, drink, an' fuck till all the money runs out."

Curly laughed. "What you care whether the nighttime whore is pretty or not?" he asked. "Hell, ugly fuck's as good as pretty, and you can't see 'em in the dark anyway."

"Enough gab," Cantrell interrupted. "It's time for you men to start earning your share. Unless I miss my guess, McMasters will be gettin' here sometime this afternoon. I don't want him gettin' no farther."

"Don't worry about that. We'll kill the son of a bitch. I told you, we got a score to settle with him," Frank said.

"Yeah? Maybe I ought to charge you for lettin' you kill him," Cantrell teased.

"Don't be funny."

"We're going to split up here. Me an' Michaels an' the woman is going to cross over into Mexico at Oro Blanco."

"Paco?" Cantrell said.

"Que?"

"Paco, I want you to take the little girl to Pajarito. If McMasters gets by Frank and Curly . . ."

"He ain't goin' to get by us, 'less we're dead," Curly said.

Cantrell studied Curly through his drooping eye for a

moment. "Yeah," he said. He turned back to Paco and continued his conversation. "If McMasters gets by Frank and Curly, I'm goin' to tell him that if anything happens to us . . . you'll kill the little girl. You can do the same thing. If he catches up with you, you let him know that if anything happens to you, I'll kill the mama. It's just a little extra insurance is all."

"*Sí*," Paco said. "If Frank and Curly kill him, *Señor* Cantrell, what do you want me to do with little girl?"

"Hell, I don't give a damn what you do with her. She's a pretty little blue-eyed blonde girl, ain't she? Don't your people like that sort of thing? If you play your cards right, you can probably sell her off somewhere."

"*Sí*, I can sell her," Paco agreed.

"No!" Millie said. "No, please, don't separate us!"

"Honey, iffen I was you, I wouldn't be worryin' 'bout that little ol' girl. You got problems of your own," Cantrell said. "By the way, Paco, maybe we'd better trade horses."

"But why, *señor*? You have a very fine *cayuse*. Your *cayuse* is *muy* better than mine."

"Yeah, well, my horse is gentle and that might make it easier for you to carry the little girl with you. And don't worry none about me gettin' the wrong end of this deal." Cantrell smiled. "Hell, I got me enough money to buy a whole horse ranch if I take a mind to."

"Yeah," Frank said. "Yeah, hey, Curly, that's what me'n you ought to do with our money. We ought to buy us a horse ranch."

"What the hell do we want a ranch for?" Curly replied. "If you own a ranch you have to work. The way I look at it, we got enough money from this job that we don't have to work no more, never.''

"Yeah, I guess you're right," Frank agreed.

"All right, get the woman back up on her horse, Michaels," Cantrell ordered. "We got to get goin'."

"Mother?" Linda called, frightened at the turn of events. "Mother, don't leave me here."

"Linda, darling, remember what I said," Millie said. "You be a big girl. Do what the man tells you, and he won't hurt you."

"Mother, I want to go with you."

"I know, darling. And I want you with me. But this won't last too long, I promise. I'll come back for you."

"Can I kiss you goodbye?" Linda asked.

"No, we ain't got time for that," Cantrell growled. "Come on, let's go."

"Your *mal de ojo*, your evil eye, is truly the mark of an evil *hombre, señor*, not to let the *bonita conchita* kiss her *mamacita adios*," Paco said.

"All right, all right, bring the brat over here and hold her up," Cantrell said. "But be quick about it."

Paco took Linda over and held her up so Millie could kiss her goodbye. As Millie's hands were tied to the pommel, she couldn't embrace her daughter, but Linda made up for it by giving her mother a big hug.

"I'll be good, Mother," Linda promised.

"I know you will, darling."

"Come on, come on," Cantrell growled. "You're breakin' my heart," he added sarcastically.

Eight

Because of his constant moving about, it wasn't every night that Boyd got to sleep in a bed. As a result he particularly enjoyed it when he could, so he was sleeping much later this morning than he normally would because this was going to be his last opportunity for a while. He had already made up his mind to leave Crittenden today.

Despite his intention to sleep late, however, the bright sun and the insistent noise of Crittenden's daily commerce spilled into his room, making sleep difficult. From somewhere nearby construction was under way, and he could hear the sound of sawing and hammering. Down the way the blacksmith was working at his forge so that the ringing sound of iron on iron could also be heard. There were other sounds as well, a freight wagon moving up the street, children playing in the schoolyard, and irritatingly, the sound of a sign squeaking in the hot, dry breeze.

Sighing in resignation, Boyd got up, poured water from the porcelain pitcher into the basin, washed his face and hands, shaved, then got dressed.

One thing he had to do before he left town was buy a horse. He had purposely put off buying a horse until the last day, so he wouldn't be responsible for paying the stall and feeding costs. He walked across the street to the livery, and saw Pete rubbing down a big chestnut.

"Mornin', Pete," he greeted pleasantly. "You must be feeling pretty good this morning. The cards went your way last night."

"They did for a fact," Pete replied, continuing the brush strokes. "You still plannin' on leavin' today?"

"I reckon so, soon as I eat breakfast and buy a horse."

"You lookin' for a horse, are you? What about this one?"

"Good-looking horse," Boyd admitted. "Who does it belong to?"

"Sam."

"You don't say."

"She won him in a poker game a couple of weeks ago," Pete explained. "She never rides him or anything. And right now he's just costin' her money for his board. I believe she'd sell him right."

Boyd examined the horse more carefully. His coat glistened like burnished copper, though his long tail was somewhat lighter. He was just under seventeen and a half hands at the withers, completely blemish free, and a model of conformation.

"I might be interested," Boyd said.

"He's a good horse," Pete went on. "He can run like the wind and he'll hold to a good trot all day without tiring."

"Maybe I'll go talk to her . . . see what she wants for him," Boyd said, patting the animal on the shoulder.

Doc came over to the stable at that moment. "Good

mornin', Captain McMasters,'' he said. "Still leaving today?"

"Yes."

"It's been a pleasure playing cards with you," Doc said. He turned toward Pete. "Listen, Pete, I'm lookin' for Rich Adams. You haven't seen him around this morning, have you?"

"No, I ain't, Doc, but then it's a little early yet. The bank don't open till nine."

"I know." Doc pulled out his pocket watch and examined it. "But Adams was supposed to meet me at eight this morning. It's half-past that now and he hasn't shown up."

"Well now, that's not hardly like Adams at all," Pete said. "He's generally a real stickler for keepin' his appointments, and he don't have much truck with other folks who don't. Maybe he's a little under the weather this mornin'. You check his house?"

"As a matter of fact I did."

"What about Mrs. Adams? What does she say?"

"Well, that's just it. I pulled on the bell cord two or three times and nobody answered." He sighed. "Well, I'm not going to worry about it. I'm sure he'll show up after a bit. Captain McMasters, good luck to you, sir. And if you ever come back this way, I hope you look us up," Doc concluded.

"I'm sure I'll be this way again," Boyd said. He pointed to the horse. "Have you fed him yet this mornin', Pete?"

"Yep."

Boyd smiled. "I'm going to talk to Sam about buying him, but remember, when he ate breakfast, he still belonged to her."

Pete chuckled. "Whatever you say," he said.

• • •

When Boyd stepped into the restaurant a moment later, he saw Sam sitting at a table near the back wall. She smiled up at him as he approached her.

"Well, come to say goodbye, have you? Sit down, join me. I don't think it would give anyone the wrong idea if we were seen having breakfast together on your last day in town."

"Especially if we were discussing business," Boyd added.

"What sort of business?"

"Horse business. The chestnut Pete was rubbing down over in the stable. He said you might want to sell it."

"One hundred and fifty dollars."

Boyd whistled. "That's a lot of money."

"I'm worth it," Sam replied, smiling sweetly.

Boyd chuckled. "Are we talking about you or the horse?"

Sam stood up, then put her hand on Boyd's. "Tell you what. Why don't you just skip breakfast and come up to my room? We'll . . . discuss it," she said, letting the last two words slide out seductively.

Sam opened the door to her room, then invited Boyd in. In the three days he had spent in Crittenden, this was the first time he had seen the inside of Sam's room. He was not prepared for what it looked like.

The room was quite large. In the middle of the room, on a raised platform, was a huge bed, covered with a deep blue silk spread. The walls were wainscoted with white painted wood on the bottom half and covered with red flocked wallpaper above. Boyd chuckled.

"What is it?"

"Your room is a little different from mine," he said.

"I live here," Sam said. "I try and make it a little more homey than an ordinary hotel room."

"Well, I would say you have succeeded," Boyd said.

"Tell me, Boyd, do we want to spend all our time discussing rooms, or horses, or . . ." She let the sentence die.

"Or what?"

"Or is there not a way we could spend our time more profitably?"

Sam walked over to her bed and turned down the covers. Then, while her back was still presented to Boyd, she began to get undressed.

Boyd had already seen her nude twice, once in the bathing room, and then again when she came to him that first night. He would have thought she had nothing left in the way of seductive teasing, but he was wrong. She managed to hold him spellbound as the smooth skin of her shoulders was exposed, then her back and then her legs until she was completely nude. She did not turn to face him, but rather raised the corner of the sheet and managed to slip into the bed without letting Boyd see more than her back. It was maddening.

"Boyd," she said, softly. "If you'll pull out the top drawer of that dresser, you'll find a robe. Please step behind the screen over there, remove your clothes, and put on the robe."

Without saying a word, Boyd took the robe over to behind the dressing screen. Quickly he removed his clothes and put on the robe, then he came back to the bed. She folded the sheet back to invite him in to be with her, giving him a modest peek at her side as she did so. He started to get in with the robe still on, and she laughed.

"Are you going to wear your robe to bed?" she asked.

"No, I guess not."

Boyd took off the robe, then slid in under the sheets. She reached over to touch him and her hand felt as if fire and ice had somehow been incorporated in the same entity.

Boyd ran his hands across her body, feeling the delightfully smooth flesh, seeing with his fingers that which the cover of the sheet denied him. His hands moved from her breasts across her flat stomach and out along the flare of her hips, then across her thighs until they found her warm, moist cleft. His fingers moved down into the gash, and slipped through the hot cream of her juices until they found the quivering little nub of flesh which sent Sam's body into convulsive chills of pleasure.

Sam's own hands were exploring Boyd's body as well, and he felt the delicate brush of her fingers as she touched and explored. Finally her hand wrapped around his penis, and he knew he could wait no longer. He rolled over her, pushing up between her legs until he found the damp yielding flesh of her sex. Sam moaned with pleasure and raised her legs up to provide him the cushion he needed.

"I am on fire inside," Sam moaned.

For a moment Boyd felt a quick sense of betrayal to Hannah. But that sense of betrayal lasted but a moment only, for he knew that he wasn't really betraying her. He had loved Hannah as he had never loved, and as he could never love another woman.

For Boyd all time was suspended, and for this moment at least, nothing else existed or mattered. There was no Cattleman's Association, there was no Protective Association, there were no outlaws threatening him. There were only the two of them, alone in the world.

Boyd went to Sam tenderly, passionately, thrusting through her swollen outer lips to plunge into the soft, inner heat. He felt her reach behind him, then pull him against her, thrusting up against him as he went deep inside to feel the rush of wet heat against his shaft.

Sam shuddered with her first climax, and Boyd thrust deeply several more times until he felt his own juices suddenly boil over and shoot out, spraying his pleasure deep inside the beautiful and spirited woman beneath him. He felt for a moment as if he were melting inside, pouring himself into Sam from the very marrow of his bones. Then, finally, he was through, and as the last spasms of pleasure washed through his own body, he felt the tiny quivers of aftershock which Sam was still enjoying. He stayed on top of her for a moment longer, then he rolled off to lie beside her. They lay together without talking for a long moment. Then Sam's hand found Boyd and she held it, tenderly.

"Must you go?" she asked.

"Yes."

"It could be good, you know. You could resign from the Association and become a full-time gambler. You're good . . . you're very good. We could go to Denver or San Francisco, or even St. Louis or New Orleans. We could make a good living together."

Boyd didn't answer.

"Who am I kidding?" Sam asked. "It wouldn't work, would it?"

"I'm sorry," Boyd said, wishing, at least for the moment, that it would.

Sam raised herself up on one elbow and looked down at Boyd. Her breasts swung like pendulums and a nipple trailed across the muscle on Boyd's forearm.

"Come," she said, smiling to change the mood. "If this is to be your last day here, let me at least buy your breakfast."

Boyd's breakfast arrived, and he had just started to eat it when there was a commotion out in the street. Immediately thereafter, someone rushed into the dining room.

"Listen, ever'body! Beckworth is runnin' up and down the street shoutin' that the bank has been robbed."

"Robbed? When? I ain't heard nor seen nothin'," one of the diners replied.

"All I know is, he's claimin' the bank has been robbed. And if anyone's got any money in there, they better get out there an' see what's goin' on."

Sam stood up. "Boyd, just about everything I have is in the bank," she said with a look of anxiousness on her face. She took in the others with a wave of her hand. "Same with everyone here."

As if validating her statement, all the diners were rushing into the street. Boyd picked up a biscuit and a couple of pieces of bacon, made himself a sandwich, then followed the others outside. The street was rapidly filling as people poured out of all the other buildings, anxious to see what was going on.

Sheriff Lindsey, who had also heard the shouting,

came out of his office to join the gathering crowd.

"Here, Beckworth, what are you shoutin' about? What's goin' on here?" Lindsey asked.

Beckworth clutched his pince-nez glasses tightly. The bow tie and high-wing collar bounced on his Adam's apple as he spoke in a high-pitched nervous voice.

"Sheriff, I just opened the bank up a few minutes ago," Beckworth said. "The first thing I always do is open the vault and take out enough money for the cash drawers so we can be about our daily business. But when I went in this morning, I discovered that the vault was empty."

"Empty!" someone gasped. "What the hell do you mean, empty?"

"I mean all the money is gone. There's nothing there."

"Goddamnit, man, my money's in there."

"Mine, too."

"So's mine."

"No," Beckworth said. "I regret to tell you, there is no money there at all."

"Where's Richard Adams?" someone demanded. "He's got some explainin' to do."

Beckworth shook his head. "I don't know. He hasn't come in yet this morning."

"He ain't come in?"

"Sheriff, listen here, you don't reckon Rich Adams has done run off with our money, do you?"

"That's it, ain't it? That's what's happened to it. That son of a bitch has run off with all the money!" someone else shouted.

"Now, hold on, hold on, there!" Lindsey said, raising his arms to quiet the agitated crowd. "I want you to stop and think about this for a minute. Rich Adams owns that big house down at the end of the street. He owns the the livery and the hotel. Now, do you really think he'd run off and leave all that behind?''

"Was the safe blowed open? Or was it opened natural?" someone asked.

"Hell, it can't be blowed open," someone else said. "Ain't that what all the struttin' was about? How this here bank had a safe that couldn't be blowed open with dynamite?"

"The safe showed no damage," Beckworth said.

"You hear that, Sheriff? No damage! Now don't that sound a little strange to you?"

Sheriff Lindsey nodded. "I'll admit, it does seem a little peculiar," he said.

"Peculiar? It's out and out suspicious."

"Where's he at, anyhow? How come he ain't out here worryin' about the bank bein' robbed if he didn't do it?"

"Just hold your horses," Lindsey said. "I'll go down to his house and talk to him."

"I'll go with you, Sheriff," Boyd said.

"Yeah, we'll all go!" one of the others shouted. "We need to show that son of a bitch he can't rob us and get away with it."

"No, we won't all go," Lindsey insisted. "The rest of you just stay right here, out of my way. There's no sense gettin' all excited about this till we know what's happened." He stroked his chin and studied Boyd for a moment. "But, Cap'n McMasters, when you get right down to it, I reckon this does sort of come under your responsibility, the bank bein' protected by the Cattleman's Protective Association an' all. Come along. If there is somethin' funny goin' on here, it would be good to have a little company.''

"Some house,'' Boyd said a moment later, as they pushed through the front gate.

"Yeah. They say he got the plans from an architect in San Francisco. I never saw a house that was designed by an architect before. Most every other house I've ever seen was just throwed up. But look at this thing, all the gee-gaws and such. Do you know it has an indoor toilet?'' He pointed to the flowers growing in colorful profusion in the front yard. "And the yard here is what you call 'landscaped.' '' He said the word slowly and distinctly. "Well, as you can see, Mrs. Adams sets quite a store by flowers and trees and shrubs and such.''

Sheriff Lindsey pulled on the bell rope and Boyd could hear the bell ringing from inside. Waiting for a moment he pulled it again, and then again.

"That's funny,'' he said. "Even if Adams wasn't here, Mrs. Adams should be.''

"Try the door,'' Boyd said.

Lindsey tried it, but it was locked. "Come on,'' he said. "We'll go around and try the back door.''

As they walked around back, Boyd saw a small bit of bright yellow cloth hanging on the back gate. He walked over to look at it while the sheriff knocked on the back door. Lindsey knocked again, then he tried the doorknob. The door swung open.

"McMasters,'' the sheriff called. "What do you think? The door's unlocked.''

Boyd left the piece of cloth untouched, then walked up to the back stoop to join Lindsey. "I think we should go in and have a look around,'' he suggested.

Cautiously, the two men stepped inside. "That sure don't look good," Lindsey said, pointing to the stove. "Pork chops, potatoes, and greens. That's a supper meal, not a breakfast."

Boyd put his hand on the stove. "I don't think the stove has been lit this morning."

"And look there," Lindsey pointed. "There's a pork chop bone on the floor. That sure isn't like Mrs. Adams. She'd never let somethin' like that stay on her floor." Lindsey pulled his pistol and started through the house. "Mr. Adams? Mr. Adams, it's me, Sheriff Lindsey. You in here?"

Not finding anyone on the first floor, the two men went up the stairs.

"Mr. Adams?" Lindsey called quietly.

Boyd saw a foot sticking out from behind a hall tree at the other end of the upstairs landing. He reached out to touch Lindsey on the shoulder. "Sheriff," he said, pointing.

The two men moved quickly over to the hall tree. "Oh, shit," Lindsey said, letting out a long sigh.

Richard Adams was on his back with his head tilted back. His mouth and eyes were wide open and there was a black hole in his forehead from which had oozed just a tiny bit of blood.

Nine

Boyd knelt down beside the body and moved one of Adams's arms, checking for rigor mortis.

"What do you think?" Lindsey asked.

"I'd say he's been dead at least six to eight hours," he said.

"Mrs. Adams and the little girl!" Lindsey said quickly. "Where are they?"

A search of the rest of the house turned up nothing. The wife and daughter were gone.

"Listen, you don't think..." Lindsey started, then he stopped, as if unable, or unwilling, to state aloud his hypothesis.

"What? That the wife might have killed him and took off with the money?" Boyd asked.

"That's what I was going to say, yes," Lindsey said. "I'd hate to think that...though in truth their marriage..." He let the word hang.

"What about their marriage?"

"Well, you met her, Cap'n. You have to admit that it was a strange one," Lindsey said. "Adams was at least twenty years older than his wife. Maybe even older. He went back East here a few years ago, not tellin' anyone what he had in mind. And when he come back, why, he was leadin' the prettiest girl you ever saw around with him. At first, some of us thought she might be a daughter that we had never heard of. You can imagine our surprise when he told everyone she was his wife.''

''Did they fight?''

''Not that I know of. She was very quiet, mostly stuck to her gardening and raising the little girl. You didn't see her out that much, and when you did see her, she seldom ever spoke. But you know what they say about still water runnin' deep.''

''She said her father was a wealthy man,'' Boyd said.

''Her father is Preston Endicott. He owns a big shipping line back in Baltimore. Most folks here don't know it, but Adams himself told me that Millie's father was so rich that it would make Adams seem like a beggar.''

''That doesn't seem like the kind of person who would kill her husband and steal fifty thousand dollars, does it?'' Boyd asked.

''No, I don't reckon it does.''

Boyd opened the doors to the chifforobe. It was full of clothes. A check of the little girl's room showed the same thing.

''She was travelling light when she left,'' Boyd said. He shook his head. ''She didn't leave willingly.''

''You tellin' me whoever killed Adams took her and the little girl?''

''Yes,'' Boyd said. He recalled the piece of cloth he had seen stuck in the gate that led out to the stable. ''Why don't we go back outside and have a look around?'' he suggested.

By the time they got downstairs, several of the townspeople had drifted down to the end of the street. They were standing in front of the house, consumed by anxious curiosity.

"What is it, Emil?" Angus Waddle called to the sheriff. "What's goin' on? Did you find Adams in there or not?"

"Yeah, what's he say about our money? Where is it?" another man shouted.

"Why don't you all just calm down?" Lindsey asked.

"We've got a right to know what's goin' on here," Angus insisted. "After all, ever'thing we got is in that bank."

"Was in it, you mean," one of the others said, and his comment was met with an angry buzz.

"I'd better go talk to 'em," Lindsey told Boyd.

Boyd began looking around the grounds while the sheriff walked out to talk to the others.

"Did you find him, Sheriff?" Pete asked.

Lindsey shook his head. "We found him," he answered.

"Well, what does he say? Where's our money?"

"He's not saying much of anything right now. He's dead."

"Dead?"

"Shot right between the eyes."

"What about Mrs. Adams and the little girl?"

"They're gone," Lindsey said.

A buzz of excitement passed through the crowd, then word was passed on to others farther back until, within minutes, word of the murder had spread through the entire town.

"What are you doin' about it?" Angus asked.

"Right now we're trying to find out as much as we can about what happened here last night."

"We?"

Lindsey pointed to Boyd. "Yes. Capatin McMasters is an officer with the Cattleman's Protective Association, don't forget. And, as of yesterday, the bank of Crittenden comes under their protection. He is on the case."

"Well, has he got any ideas?"

"Give him time, will you? Give us both time," Lindsey pleaded. He turned then, and walked back toward the stable.

When he got there, Boyd handed him the piece of yellow cloth. "Did Mrs. Adams do her own sewing?"

"No," Lindsey answered. "Mrs. Pinchot did her sewin'. Mrs. Pinchot does the sewin' for most of the women in town."

"See if she recognizes this cloth," Boyd said. "I found it hanging in the gate over there."

"Did you find anything else?"

Boyd pointed to the ground. "Two horses came in here, three left. Looks like one of them was being led. See how close this set of prints follows that set? Whoever is riding this horse is holding the reins of this one."

"That would be the horse Millie is on," Lindsey said. "Damn, who could do a thing like this?"

"His name is Cantrell. Cantrell robbed the bank and took the woman and child."

"What?" Lindsey asked in surprise. "How do you know that?"

"During the train holdup the other night, I heard one of the robbers yell at another one who remained in the dark. The robber who remained in the dark was called Cantrell."

"But what has that to do with this?"

"Cantrell was one of the ones who got away." He

pointed to the tracks of the horse that was leading the other. "This was the horse Cantrell was riding. I saw the prints that night. Look. Do you see the tie-bar shoe?"

Lindsey nodded. "I can see how that might make you suspicious, Cap'n, but when you get right down to it, there's probably at least one tie-bar ever' hundred horses or so. I'm not sure something like this would ever hold up in court."

"I don't need to take the son of a bitch to court," Boyd said. "All I have to do is find him. And all the other tie-bars aren't like this one. This one has a crescent cut in the top. Take a closer look and you'll see what I mean."

"I'll be damned," Lindsey said, bending down to examine the shoe more closely. "Yeah, now that you point it out, I do see."

"No!" a woman suddenly screamed, running through the crowd, coming toward Boyd and the sheriff. When Boyd looked over, he was surprised to see that the screaming woman was Sam.

"Where is she?" Sam shouted. "Where is Linda?" She started toward the house.

"Sam! Sam, stop, don't go in there!" Lindsey called out.

Sam stopped and looked around. Tears were streaming down her face. "Where is she, Emil? Where is my Linda?"

"Linda? Isn't that the little girl?" Boyd asked, confused by Sam's strange reaction.

"You've got to find her," Sam insisted. She looked at Boyd. "Boyd, that is your job, isn't it? Go look for her. You can find her, I know you can."

"Sam, I'm going to do everything I can," Boyd started, but before he could finish his sentence, Sam interrupted him.

"You want my horse? Take him, no charge. I'll give him to you free."

"You don't have to do that. I'll pay a fair price for him."

"I want to do it. I'll do anything to get Linda back safely."

"I didn't realize you thought so much of Mrs. Adams's little girl," Boyd said.

"Mrs. Adams's little girl? Boyd, don't you understand? Linda is *my* daughter! Mine and Richard Adams's! Please, you must find her! Oh, what kind of beasts are these? How could anyone do such a thing?"

How could anyone? Boyd thought. He remembered his wife, Hannah. A group of no-count outlaws, the Winslow brothers, captured her and held her hostage in his own house, demanding that he meet their demands or they would kill Hannah and burn the house. Desperate to protect his wife, Boyd gave in to the Winslow brothers' demands. But they didn't keep their end of the bargain. Tying Hannah to the bed, they set fire to the house, burning her alive. Boyd arrived in time to see the flames and hear his wife's dying screams, but not in time to save her.

Boyd made the Winslows pay for their satanic deed. They paid with their lives. But he could still hear his wife's screams, and he could still see the vision of her through the flames, tied helplessly to the bed. That memory, he knew, had just been reawakened by this man

Cantrell. Cantrell had taken Mrs. Adams and the little girl as his hostage.

In Boyd's mind it was easy for Millicent Adams to become Hannah, and for the little girl to be the child that Hannah so desperately wanted, but had not lived long enough to have. Boyd knew nothing about Cantrell but his name. But Cantrell had just become the Winslows to him. And that meant that the son of a bitch had to die.

He looked at Sam. His face was set and his eyes were black. He nodded.

"I'll find her," he said.

"The horse is yours," Sam said. "I'll bring a bill of sale to you."

As Boyd started back toward the stable, word quickly spread that he was going after the robbers and kidnappers.

"Bring the bastards back, belly down," someone shouted.

"We're for you, Cap'n!" another added.

The crowd parted for him as he made his way to the depot to pick up his saddle. He didn't have to carry the saddle to the stable, because Pete walked the horse down to him. Angus was with Pete.

"Captain McMasters," Angus said. "I want to apologize about that first night you was here. What I did was way out of line."

"All right, no harm done," Boyd said. He threw the saddle onto the horse.

"Sheriff Lindsey tells me that you believe Jason Cantrell did this," Angus continued.

Boyd looked at Angus with interest. "Jason Cantrell?" he said. "Do you know him?"

"He's been in my store a few times."

"Can you describe him?"

"I'd say he's a medium-sized fella. Sandy-haired. Pock-faced. And he's got a eye that sorta droops. You know what I mean? His . . ." Angus put his hand up to his own eye. "His left eyelid looks like it's half-closed. That's Cantrell. He runs with a fella named Michaels, so if there was two of 'em here last night, chances are the other one was Michaels. Michaels is a bit bigger than Cantrell. He's got kind of a round face, and a nose that looks like it was broken, maybe more than once."

"Thanks," Boyd said.

Sam came up to them then, carrying a piece of paper. "Here it is," she said. "The bill of sale."

Boyd put some money into her hand. "And here is the hundred and fifty dollars you were asking."

Sam looked at the money, then smiled. She gave him fifty dollars back. "All right," she said. "Let's compromise. If you're going to pay, pay a fair price. After our . . . negotiations this morning . . . I was willing to take one hundred."

Boyd chuckled. "That's funny. After our negotiations I was willing to pay the full amount."

Pete watched the exchange between the two, not quite sure what was going on, but with the feeling that they weren't talking just about the horse.

"I didn't lie to you about the horse," Pete said. "He'll get you there and back."

"Cap'n McMasters!" Emil Lindsey called out. He was coming up the street in long, quick strides. A stout middle-aged woman was hurrying behind the sheriff, practically running to keep up with him. "Cap'n McMasters, wait a moment. This here is Mrs. Pinchot."

"Who?"

"Pinchot. You remember, the seamstress?"

"Oh, yes," Boyd said. "Mrs. Pinchot, did you recognize the cloth?"

"Indeed, I did. The swatch of material the sheriff showed me was from a riding-habit I made for Mrs. Adams," Mrs. Pinchot said. "In style, it is a princess dress of yellow, closed in front with buttons and button holes from the neck to the hem. Opening the buttons from the hem will allow the skirt to be split at the bottom for riding. On the left side is a pocket. The collar and cuffs of the dress are of fine blue linen. I have a drawing here," she offered, handing him a piece of paper.

Boyd looked at it, then put it and the piece of cloth into his shirt pocket. "Thank you, ma'am," he said. "This will be most helpful."

"I do hope you find her and the child. Mrs. Adams is a very quiet and shy woman. But when you can get through her shyness, you will discover that she is a most delightful person."

Boyd recalled his brief conversation with her during the ceremony at the bank. Everyone was talking about what a pretty woman she was, and that was true. But there was a vulnerability to her as well, and Boyd found that he had been drawn as much toward that as he had her looks.

"I'll find her, Mrs. Pinchot," Boyd promised. What he thought, but didn't say, either to Mrs. Pinchot or to Sam, was that he hoped he could find her before it was too late.

Ten

After leaving the others, Cantrell, Michaels, and Millie travelled all day, dismounting occasionally to, in Cantrell's words, "give the horses a blow." Even then they didn't stop, but continued to walk, always putting distance behind them. They did pause briefly when the sun was straight overhead in order to eat a few bites of jerky and to take a few swallows of water.

Michaels chewed on the leathery jerky, then took a drink of tepid water from his canteen. He spit some out in disgust, and wiped his mouth with the back of his hand.

"Goddamn water tastes like horse piss," he complained. "And the jerky tastes like dog turds. We ought not to be eatin' this shit. We ought to be eatin' steak an' drinkin' beer. There's got to be a town near here. Listen, Cantrell, don't you think there's a town around here somewhere?"

"What if there is?"

"Well, if there is, I was thinkin' we could go in an' get somethin' fit to eat an' decent to drink," Michaels said. He giggled. "I mean, it ain't like we don't have any money."

"You was thinkin', was you? What makes you believe you have enough brains to think?"

"You got no right to talk to me like that, Cantrell."

Cantrell looked over at Michaels, then he sighed. "Look, I've done right by you so far, ain't I? Have I made any mistakes yet?"

"No, I don't reckon you have."

"Then just do what I say for a little while longer and things will be fine," Cantrell insisted. "We can't go into town yet. We're still too close to Crittenden. By now they've prob'ly sent out telegrams all aroun'. If we show up with a woman prisoner and a bag full of money, what do you think's goin' to happen?"

Michaels thought for a moment, then he smiled. "Folks is goin' to know we was the ones that robbed the bank."

"That's right. We'll go into town when it's safe to go into town," Cantrell said. "I want to put a couple of days between us and Crittenden."

"All right, all right," Michaels agreed. "Only it don't hardly seem right to be half starvin' to death when we got more money here than we ever had in our lives."

"Look at her," Cantrell said. "You don't see her complainin', do you?"

Millie had eaten her little strip of jerky and drunk the water without complaint, grateful, at this point, to even still be alive.

Cantrell screwed the cap back on his canteen, then hooked it back onto his saddle. "Mount up," he said. He walked over to Millie's horse, and when she was remounted, he tied her hands to the pommel again. That done, he mounted himself, took the line from Millie's horse, and they started riding once more.

"How far are we goin', Cantrell?" Michaels asked.

"As far as it takes," Cantrell answered.

Several miles behind them, Boyd dismounted and looked around. He had followed the tracks to an arroyo where he found evidence of a camp. There was a burned-out campfire and coffee grounds on the dirt where the last dregs of coffee had been poured. Examining the horse droppings, he concluded that the camp had been maintained for at least twenty-four hours or so. Also, according to the signs, three riders had waited here while two more went into town. Three riders came back from town, then three went south and three went southwest. The tie-bar shoe that he had been following went southwest.

Boyd remounted and started to go southwest after the tie-bar shoe when something caught his attention. He turned back, then dismounted to examine the droppings of one of the horses that went west.

That horse had been eating oats.

He smiled. The horse Millie Adams was riding had been eating oats. The other horses had been eating hay. The tie-bar went southwest, but Millie Adams's horse went west. Her horse went west, but did she? Or did one of the other men take a shine to her horse and take it from her?

Boyd twisted around in his saddle to look back in the direction of the southwest-bound tracks, trying to make up his mind which way to go, when a rifle cracked, and he heard the deadly whine of a bullet frying the air right by his head. Luckily he had just changed positions in his saddle at almost exactly the same moment the rifle was fired. Had he not done this, he would be dead.

Boyd leaped out of the saddle, snaking his rifle out

of the boot as he did so. He slapped the horse on the rump to get it out of the line of fire, then he ran, zigzagging, toward a little knoll. Another bullet hit the dirt just after he zigged, and it whined away into the desert. Boyd dived for the top of the knoll then rolled over to the other side. He turned around then and inched back up to peek over the top.

He saw no one.

Boyd slipped back down, then he put his hat on the end of his rifle and poked it up over the edge of the knoll. He held it there for a long moment, hoping to draw fire, but nothing happened. Then, when he was absolutely certain that there was no one there, he moved cautiously to where the ambusher had been.

Whoever had been there was gone, but Boyd found the remains of a quirly cigarette, and the spent brass casing of a .44-40 jacked out of the rifle by the assailant after firing. He also saw horse tracks nearby, leading off to the southwest.

"All right," Boyd said aloud. "So now I know which set of tracks to follow. I'm going southwest."

That was easier said than done. His horse had spooked under fire and it took Boyd more than half an hour to find him. He was beginning to think that he was going to have a long, hot dry walk back into town, when he saw the horse standing quietly down in a ravine.

"Hey, horse," Boyd said. "Where the hell have you been, you dumb bastard? When I slap you on the rump like that, all I want you to do is to get the hell out of the way. I don't mean go off and leave me."

Boyd remounted, then started after the tracks heading southwest.

•   •   •

Though Boyd didn't look up, there was a hawk high overhead. While Boyd headed southwest, the hawk veered toward the south, flying over, though not consciously following, the south-bound set of tracks. Had the hawk followed the tracks for an hour at his swift speed, he would have seen three horses making a slow progress across the desert.

Cantrell, Michaels, and Millie had just finished their lunch and were continuing west even as Boyd started southwest. With every passing minute now, the distance was widening between them.

The three rode and walked through the rest of the afternoon, continuing on through the long shadows of sunset. Then, as the last twilight faded, Cantrell held up his hand to signal the others to stop.

"We may as well tie down here 'n' sleep a spell," Cantrell said. "By my figurin' we got at least eight or ten hours head start on anyone who might be comin' after us and they ain't goin' to be able to track us in the dark."

"You heard what they was sayin' about McMasters, didn't you?" Michaels said. "He can track 'most like a Indian."

"If the Dobbs boys done their job like they're supposed to, McMasters is already dead." Cantrell giggled. "And if he ain't dead, he's goin' to be in for a surprise when he tracks down that tie-bar shoe."

"Son of a bitch! That's why you changed horses with Paco, ain't it?" Michaels said. "I figured maybe your horse had gone lame or somethin'."

"Yeah, well, Paco probably figured that, too," Cantrell said. "And by the time he realized the horse wasn't goin' lame, he was so glad about it that he didn't even consider anything else . . . like maybe he was ridin' the horse McMasters would be followin'.''

Michaels laughed. ''I got to hand it to you, that was pretty smart of you, throwin' McMasters off our trail like that.''

''Yeah, I thought it was pretty smart of me, too,'' Cantrell bragged.

''We stayin' the night here?''

Cantrell looked around. ''This looks like about as good a place as any,'' he said.

''Good, I'm pretty tired. But first I gotta take me a piss,'' Michaels said. ''Ooops, sorry, lady,'' he said.

Cantrell laughed.

''What you laughin' at?''

''You apologizin' for sayin' you have to take a piss.''

''Womenfolk like it when men are polite,'' Michaels said. ''Don't you know that?''

''What do I care what womenfolk like? I ain't never had a woman I didn't pay for, and if I pay for her, then seems to me like it's her job to do what I like. Don't you think that's right, little lady?'' he asked Millie.

Millie, who was hanging on the edge of hysterical exhaustion, was barely able to hear their conversation. ''Please,'' she said quietly. ''Please, just untie me and let me get down.''

''Sure thing, honey, don't mean to discomfort you none more'n we have to,'' Cantrell said easily. He walked over and released her bonds and Millie, with a grateful sigh, slipped down from the horse. She walked over to sit in a patch of soft sand beneath a large saguaro cactus. Except for the times they walked their horses, and the short break when they rendezvoused with the other outlaws at the arroyo, she had been riding now for almost eighteen hours. Never, in her life, had she been so long on a horse. She let her head hang forward.

"Don't you be gettin' none too comfortable, yet, girlie," Cantrell said. "I got plans for you." He started unbuttoning his pants. "Yes, ma'am, me an' you is goin' to have some fun."

When Millie saw him coming toward her, her fear became palpable, and she felt bile in her throat. "No," she said in a choked voice. "No, please don't. You told the other man that I was for insurance."

"Hell, honey, I just told 'im that so he wouldn't touch you," Cantrell said. "I wanted the first crack at you myself, that's all."

"No," Millie whimpered. "Please, no."

Millie squeezed her eyes shut, trying, unsuccessfully to prevent the tears from sliding down her cheeks. Her entreaties fell upon deaf ears however, for she felt him approaching, then she smelled his foul breath and the body stench of him as he knelt down beside her.

"Go ahead and cry if you want to, girlie," Cantrell said, putting his hands on her shoulder and pushing her back. "I like it when you cry."

Millie fell back, and, in an instant, Cantrell was on top of her. He put one of his hands in the open area caused by the unbuttoned riding habit, then slid it up the inside of her thigh. When he reached the junction of her legs, he stopped, and looked at her in surprise.

"Well I'll be a son of a bitch!" he gasped. "Michaels, guess what I'm feelin' up here?"

"What?" Michaels asked.

"Nothin'," Cantrell said. He laughed. "I ain't feelin' nothin' a'tall, 'ceptin' pussy hair. This here woman is naked as a jaybird under this garment."

"You lyin' to me?" Michaels asked.

"Not a bit. By god, girl, you're wantin' this, ain't you?"

"No!" Millie said sharply. "No, please! I was afraid! You . . . you told me to hurry. You said if Linda and I weren't dressed within five minutes, you would kill us. I didn't take the time to put on any lingerie."

"Well, whatever the reason, if I don't have to bother to take off a bunch of undergarments, it's goin' to make doin' this a lot easier."

"No," Millie said. "You have the money. You've got what you want. You don't have to do this."

"Oh yeah, I do have to do this," Cantrell replied. "Fact is, I been wantin' to do this ever since I seen them little titties of yours pokin' through that thin silk nightgown. Now you got two ways of gettin' through this. You can either cry an' fight me . . . and I got to tell you, honey, I like that. I like that a lot. Or, you can do like the whores do, pretendin' that you like it, even though you don't. However you do it is up to you."

Millie closed her eyes and bit her lower lip as she felt his calloused hands bunching up her riding skirt sliding it up to either side of her naked legs until she could feel night air on the most intimate parts of her body. She held her legs together as tightly as she could.

"Damn if I don't kinda wish I'd made you keep on that little silk sleepin' gown you was wearin' when I first seen you," Cantrell said. "I tell you the truth, that give me such a hard-on I though I was goin' to bust." He laughed, demonically. " 'Course, that was before I cut it up like I done."

Millie felt Cantrell drop his pants, then she felt his

hands between her thighs, forcing her to spread her legs apart. She gasped.

"There, that's a good girl," Cantrell grunted.

Millie felt Cantrell's weight press against her bruised, racked body. That was followed by a stabbing, invasive pain and she knew he was in her.

Remembering the two options he had given her, one to fight and the other to pretend she was enjoying it, she chose, instead, a third. She lay in absolute silence, without making the slightest move, while above her, he grunted and thrust, and squealed like a pig.

Fortunately, the attack was incredibly brief. In less than one minute Cantrell had satisfied himself, and after a few more grunts and groans, he pulled himself from her, then collapsed beside her, breathing heavily.

"Goddamn, girlie, that was about the sorriest fuck I ever had," he growled. "Ain't no one ever learned you what to do? I've had fifty-year-old whores that was better'n that. How can you just lay there without no movin' or no sound a'tall?"

Cantrell pulled his pants on, then walked over a few feet to relieve himself loudly.

"Michaels, you want some of that?" he asked.

"I reckon so," Michaels said. He had been sitting under a tree, watching. "I got me a hard-on while I was watchin'."

"You did? Damn, you prob'ly enjoyed it more'n I did, then," Cantrell said. He buttoned his pants, then made a motion toward her. "Go ahead, do it," he said. "But be sure'n tie her up when you get finished."

Millie steeled herself for one more ordeal. It didn't hurt quite as much this time as it did the first, and, for a moment, she wondered why. Then she realized that though her natural juices hadn't made her slick, the result of Cantrell's rape had. And though she was sickened to think of his foul seed inside her, she was, nevertheless, grateful for the lubricant it provided.

If anything, Michaels completed the operation even more quickly than Cantrell had, having just penetrated her when, with a gasp and a long moan, he was finished. He pulled himself out, then collapsed beside her, breathing heavily.

Eleven

It was quiet. It had been several minutes now since Michaels collapsed alongside Millie. She looked over at him and saw that his eyes were closed. She held her breath and prayed a silent prayer. When he finished, he had forgotten to tie her up again. Perhaps he would fall asleep without doing it! Cantrell was already snoring, stretched out beside a rock about thirty feet away.

Millie lay very still. This was difficult for her to do for the residue of their lust was running down her thigh and she convulsed to think of it. But she made no move for fear of disturbing Michaels, who lay there with his eyes closed, still breathing heavily.

After several moments, Michaels's breathing grew more measured, and Millie was ready to believe that he was asleep. She sat up, moving very quietly, and looked at him. Yes, she thought, nearly shouting with joy at her unexpected good luck. Yes, he was asleep!

Millie started tiptoeing toward her horse. Once she heard one of the men snort and roll over and she stopped, frozen in fear. But she wasn't discovered.

She reached the horses and, very quietly, untied her own. "Be very quiet, Dandy," she whispered, for the horse they had taken for her was, by coincidence, her favorite riding horse. His name was Dandy and he had been bred in Virginia and shipped out to Arizona as a gift from her father.

For a moment she thought of taking their horses with her as well, but she was afraid that in attempting to take them, she would make too much noise, so she abandoned that plan. She led her horse over one hundred yards away into the darkness, then she climbed onto his back and rode off.

She had escaped!

"Linda," she said under her breath. "Hold on, darling. I'm coming to get you!"

She thought about her daughter as she rode through the night, wondering if she was safe.

Her daughter.

Of course, Linda wasn't really her daughter. That is, she was not biologically Millie's daughter. But the baby had come to her within the first few hours of her birth, and as far as Linda knew, Millie was her mother.

Millie knew this. She loved the child as dearly as she could possibly love one of her own.

Linda was actually the baby of Samantha Chance, the lady gambler. Samantha claimed that she didn't know who the father was, but Millie had come to believe that it was Richard.

Millie didn't hold it against Richard. In fact, she rather appreciated his sense of obligation toward the child. And Samantha had been very sweet about it. For though she did visit Linda occasionally, she had never made the first move toward trying to assert any type of claim, actual or emotional, toward the child.

For his part, Richard had made no effort to give Millie

her own baby. In five years of marriage, Millie could count on her hands the times they had been together as husband and wife. He had come to her a few times early in their marriage, but his visits had been half-hearted even then, and more often than not, they had ended in impotent frustration.

Richard's visits across the hall grew fewer and fewer, until the last year, when he didn't come at all.

Millie would wait quietly in her bed, listening, hoping for a visit from her husband, all to no avail. Then, as night after night passed with no footfalls in the hallway, she abandoned all hope that he would ever come again on his own. She tried a few times to entice him over. She even made the very silk gown that Cantrell referred to, in the hopes that it would do the trick. And she had stepped over to his bedroom several times on one pretext or another trying, without success, to arouse his interest.

Now, as she rode through the darkness, hurting and bespoiled by the filth of the two despicable men, she wondered how she could have ever thought such an act between a man and woman could be pleasureable.

But no, she must not think like that, she told herself. With the right man it could be wonderful. She had to hold on to that belief. To believe that she would never again know the pleasure she had known with Adrian was, unthinkable.

Millie thought of Adrian . . . Captain Adrian Kent. He had been the master of one of her father's ships. How he had loved her, and how she had loved him. With him, she had known the pleasure a man and woman could share.

And with him she had known scandal. For she discovered that she was pregnant while he was on a voyage around the Horn to San Francisco.

Actually, she had been deliriously happy when she first discovered that she was pregnant, for she knew that the objections her father had raised to their marriage would, of necessity, be eliminated when Adrian returned. Her father would have no choice but to sanction, and even bless the marriage of his daughter to his youngest and boldest sea captain.

But Captain Adrian Kent did not return from his last voyage. He drowned when his ship foundered in heavy seas while rounding the Horn, and when Millie heard the tragic news, she was so distraught that she miscarried. It was not until the miscarriage that anyone else knew of her condition.

The doctor who treated Millie during her difficult miscarriage, could not wait to tell his wife of "the scandal of 'the daughter of one of Baltimore's most important men being pregnant out of wedlock.' " His wife, armed with the juiciest bit of gossip of the season, eagerly spread the word.

Within a week, Millie Endicott, who, that very year, had been declared in a story printed in the *Baltimore Sun* as "The most desirable debutante in all Baltimore," became a social pariah, an outcast confined to her father's home. For the next several weeks, she stayed in her room with the curtains drawn, unable to face anyone because of the shame and dishonor she had brought upon herself and upon her family.

It was during her time of self-imposed confinement that Richard Adams arrived in Baltimore on a business trip. When Preston Endicott learned that Adams was from far-off Arizona, he conceived of the idea of relocating Millie to Arizona, thus getting his daughter "out of sight, out of mind.'' He settled a very generous sum of money, which he euphemistically called a ''dowry,'' on Richard Adams to entice him to marry Millie.

Millie was still too heartbroken over the loss of her one true love to protest the marriage her father had arranged for her. There was nothing in Baltimore for her anymore, anyway. If her father wanted her to marry this man who was, himself, as old as her father, then so be it.

That was over five years ago, and Millie had not seen her father since. As she rode through the darkness on her desperate escape, she wondered if she would ever see him . . . or anyone else . . . again.

Millie was riding in a southeasterly direction, not only trying to escape from the awful men who had captured her and used her, but also moving in a direction that she believed would take her to Pajarito. Had she applied geometry to a map of the area, she would have seen that she was in the process of making a second leg to a triangle. The first leg had been made during the day as she had been taken by Cantrell and Michaels toward the Mexican Border. Her escape route formed the second leg.

About ten miles southeast of Millie's present location, Boyd McMasters was closing the third leg of the triangle, though neither he nor Millie knew this. Boyd had tracked the three horses he was following to the eastern bank of the eastern branch of the Santa Cruz River. There, he dismounted and looked at the river, now a gleaming thread of silver in the moonlight.

According to the sign he was reading, the three people he was tracking had entered the river here. Boyd knew, though, that they could have gone north or south for quite a ways before coming out on the other side and, in the dark, he could easily lost their trail.

With a reluctant sigh, he decided this would be as good a place as any to spend the night, so he walked back to his horse and untied his bedroll.

"You goin' to be here when I wake up in the morning, Horse?" he asked. The horse whickered and looked at him.

Boyd chuckled. "Yeah, you tell me that now, but what happened to you this afternoon?" he asked. "I'll just have to see how loyal you are in the morning."

Boyd built a campfire and started some coffee. Then, while waiting for his coffee, he pulled a little sack filled with brass carpet tacks from his saddlebag. He dumped the contents of the sack onto the blanket and examined the tacks, gleaming by the light of the fire.

He noticed that he was running low, and figured he would have to buy some more the next time he was around a mercantile.

Boyd's trademark was the grievous wounds his bullets inflicted upon his victims. It was those wounds, in fact, that caused some outlaws to refer to him as "Bullet."

Many thought they could understand how his rifle did so much damage. The size of the bullet was enough to generate an enormous amount of energy. But no one understood why the bullets from his pistol could also do such things as leave ten holes and shatter an arm bone, totally mangle a leg so that it was impossible to repair, or blow off an arm. That was a secret that Boyd had told no one.

Boyd emptied a box of .44-caliber cartridges onto the blanket alongside the carpet tacks. Then, one by one, he

began pressing the brass tacks into the soft lead noses
of the bullets. The heads of the tacks were about a third
of an inch across and the nail part sunk into the lead
better than half an inch. When a bullet so modified
struck its target, the brass head of the tack would then
penetrate while the soft lead would fragment and fly in
all directions.

This was precisely what had given him such a killing
advantage when he trapped first the Andersons and then
the Dobbses against the side of the cliff wall. One of
these bullets striking a sheer rock wall would instantly
shatter into eight or ten deadly missiles.

Boyd worked quickly and expertly until he had all the
bullets modified. He didn't have to do anything to the
bullets in his guns. They were already doctored.

After Boyd had his bullets prepared, he drank his coffee and ate a piece of jerky. Then he laid out his bedroll.
He put the piece of canvas down, then the blanket, then
the saddle, trailing the stirrups down along the blanket.
Finally he covered the saddle with another blanket and
put his hat at the head.

When Boyd was through, he moved about twenty
yards away, slipped down into a little depression, and
looked back upon his handiwork. The fire was burning
low, the area smelled of coffee, the horse stood quietly
over in the dark, while, on the bedroll, a hat covered
what appeared to be the head of a sleeping man. The
saddle made a perfect dummy. Satisfied with the illusion
he had created, he settled back to wait.

Boyd extracted a cigarillo and stuck it in his mouth,
wishing he could light it. He got some satisfaction just
by sucking air through the tobacco, but it wasn't equal

to a good smoke. He sat there in the dark with his gaze sweeping back and forth, looking for any movement.

Paco, Frank, and Curly had crossed the river together. Paco, as instructed by Cantrell, did not stop, but went on to Pajarito. Curly and Frank continued on for three miles beyond the river, then they climbed up onto a promontory and looked back toward the east to see if they could spot the man who was so relentlessly dogging their trail.

Frank was berating Curly.

" 'Let me take care of him,' you said. 'There's nothin' to it,' you said. So I let you go back to bushwhack him and what happens? You let him get away. He's still on our tail," Frank said.

"I don't understand it. I had him dead in my sights," Curly replied. "I don't know how I could have missed him."

"I don't know how you could have missed him either, but you did, and the son of a bitch is still comin' after us."

"I'll tell you what I don't understand. There were two sets of tracks leavin' the campsite. What'd he choose ours for? If he had gone the other way, he wouldn't be our problem."

"Yeah, and if a frog had wings he wouldn't bump his ass ever' time he jumped," Frank said. "He did come this way, and he is our problem."

"It's dark now. Maybe we can lose him."

"How we goin' to lose him? The son of a bitch can't be lost. No, sir, the only way we're goin' to get shed of him is to kill him."

"I tried that, remember? It didn't work."

"You didn't try hard enough."

"You want him dead, you kill him," Curly suggested.

"Why don't we both do it? That's what we're gettin' paid for. We can cut back on our own trail. He's not goin' to track us in the dark, so you know the son of a bitch is goin' to have to bed down somewhere. And since he's trailin' us, it'll be easy enough for us to find him. All we have to do is locate his camp, sneak up on him in the night, and shoot the son of a bitch while he's sleepin'."

"All right," Curly relented. "Let's do it and be done with it."

With Paco now more than two miles ahead of them, Curly and Frank turned their horses around and started following back along their own trail. Frank saw the campfire first.

"Curly, look!" he said, pointing. "There's a campfire on the other side of the river."

"Would you look at that?" Curly said. "Why the hell would he build a fire like that?"

" 'Cause he didn't figure on our comin' back on him, that's why," Frank replied, laughing out loud. "We done it, Curly! We've got 'im!"

"That's what I thought today, too," Curly said. "But the slippery son of a bitch got away."

"Why don't we just see how slippery the son of a bitch can be with a couple of bullets in his gut? He ain't goin' to get away this time, I guarantee it."

The two men dismounted and tied off their horses, then they crossed the river on foot.

"You stay back here," Frank whispered.

"Why?"

"You had your chance at him this afternoon. Now it's my time."

"That ain't fair. He was awake this afternoon. He's asleep now."

"That don't make no never-mind. You had your chance, now this is mine."

"All right, all right," Curly said. "As long as the bastard is dead, I don't really care much who kills him."

Curly waited down by the river as Frank started toward the campfire, a small, dim blaze that was now some fifty yards away. He watched until his brother was completely swallowed up by darkness.

It had been a long, tiring trail. As a result Boyd, who was tired, dozed off several times during the night. But even while he was asleep he was alert, and when, while approaching the campsite, Frank's foot dislodged a pebble, Boyd was instantly awake. By the light of the moon, Boyd saw someone approaching the "sleeping" saddle.

Boyd raised his gun and watched and waited.

The night intruder pulled his pistol out and pointed it toward the bedroll. He took careful aim, then fired twice. The muzzle flash of his pistol lit up the night, the booming sound of the shots echoed back from this hills.

"Curly! Curly, I got him!" Frank shouted loudly.

"Sorry Frank. I'm afraid you missed again," Boyd said easily.

"What the hell?" Frank shouted, spinning around and blazing away in the direction of the sound of Boyd's voice.

Boyd returned fire so quickly that the boom of his pistol covered the boom of Frank's. And yet that was only an illusion, for Boyd had delayed his own shot long enough to be able to use the flame pattern of Frank's muzzle-blast as his target. Boyd fired only once, but that was all he needed. Frank dropped his gun, then crumpled.

"Frank! Frank!" Curly called from the darkness. "What's happenin', Frank?"

"I just killed Frank, Curly," Boyd said. "You'd better come on in and give yourself up."

"Like hell I will!" Curly called back from the darkness.

Boyd heard, but could not see, Curly running over rocky ground. Boyd knew when Curly hit the river because he heard water splashing. He looked toward the sound, trying to see Curly. Although he couldn't see Curly, he could see the little fluorescent feathers of white water kicked up by Curly's feet as he splashed across the shallow river. Boyd fired a couple of times in the general direction of the white splashes, but Curly was too far away and it was too dark for him to have a real target.

Once Curly reached the other side of the river the white splashes disappeared, and he became invisible again. A moment after Curly left the river, Boyd heard the scrape of iron horseshoe on hard rock and he knew that Curly had mounted. The retreating drum of hoofbeats told him that Curly had gotten away.

Boyd's horse was not saddled, so he made no effort to go after Curly. Instead he returned to the crumpled form of the man he had shot. He could see the man's stomach wound clearly, a wide spread of blood, gleaming dully in the in the moonlight.

"You was wrong when you said you'd killed me," the man said, straining to talk.

"No," Boyd replied easily. "I wasn't wrong. I might have been a little early, but I wasn't wrong. I have killed you."

"We shoulda kept on ridin' when we had the chance."

"It wouldn't have done any good. I would've found you," Boyd said.

"Yeah, I guess so."

"Where's the woman and the little girl, Frank?"

Frank coughed. "You think I'm goin' to tell you that?"

"You may as well."

"To hell with you, you son of a bitch," Frank swore. "You the one that killed Matt and Luke. You the one that took me an' Curly to jail. And now you the one that killed me. Not tellin' you what you want to know is about the only way I got of gettin' one over on you."

"All right," Boyd said, easily. "I'll find them without you. How you want your name to read? Do you have a middle name or initial you want me to use?"

Frank coughed. "Use for what?" he asked. "What are you talkin' about?"

"It's for your grave marker."

"Ha! What grave marker?"

"The one I'm about to make for you," Boyd said. "You see, I'm goin' to bury you right here where you lie," Boyd explained. "I'm going to write your name on a piece of paper and stick it into an empty shell casing, then I'm going push that casing down into the dirt over your grave."

Frank tried to laugh, but his laughter turned into convulsive coughs. "You're funny, mister. You know that?" he said.

"I'm just making the offer."

"Yeah? Well, don't bother. Truth to tell, I don't know if I got a middle name or not. Hell, I don't even know what my real last name is. Ma called us both Dobbs, 'cause that's what she called herself. But she was a whore . . . didn't even know who our papas was."

"Frank, are the woman and the girl still alive?" Boyd asked.

Frank started coughing. "Could I have some water? I got me a powerful thirst. Give me some water and I'll tell you what I know."

Boyd walked over to get his canteen. He knew about this, about the terrible dryness in the throat just before a man died. He had given quite a few men their last drink of water. Oftentimes they were men he had killed.

Boyd knelt down and handed his canteen to Frank. Frank took several desperate swallows, making gurgling sounds as he drank.

"They was still alive last time I saw 'em," Frank said.

"Where are they?"

"It's quit hurtin'."

"What?"

"My gut. It don't hurt no more." Frank laughed. "You know, maybe I'm not goin' to die after all. Maybe I'm goin' to get up and walk away from here. Ain't that goin' to be a good one on you?"

"Frank? Frank, where are the woman and the little girl?"

There was no answer.

"Frank?"

Boyd put his hand on Frank's neck. There was no pulse. When he moved his hand down to find Frank's heart, he found a packet of money. Unbuttoning his shirt, he found two more packets of money, plus a judge's gavel. He also found a packet of money in each pocket.

The total came to ten thousand dollars.

Boyd stood up and took the money and his canteen over to his saddle. Then he pulled out a small spade and began digging. The ground was fairly easy to dig here, and within half an hour he had a hole deep enough to roll Frank down into. He closed the grave, then he poked out the empty shell casing from his .44. This was the casing that held the propellent and bullet that killed Frank.

Taking a pencil and a piece of paper, Boyd wrote:

Frank Dobbs,
Murderer, Rapist,
and
Bank Robber
Escaped from a legally
ordered hanging in
New Mexico,
run down,
killed and
brought to final justice
on Sept. 7th, 1881
by
Captain Boyd McMasters
of the
Cattleman's Protective Association
in the lawful performance
of his duty.

Twelve

Pajarito

It was about ten o'clock at night when Paco rode into Pajarito. He went directly to the Casa de Sol Cantina, dismounted, then helped the little girl down.

"Paco, the girl is too young for you," someone shouted in Spanish. "How can you fuck such a little girl? Your cock is as big as she is."

"You have an evil tongue, my friend," Paco replied. "You should be careful that someone does not cut it from your mouth."

"Will my mother be here?" Linda asked.

"No, little one. Not now," Paco said.

"I'm hungry," Linda said.

"Come inside. I will get something for you to eat."

Paco and Linda went inside, then Paco guided her to a table near the wall.

"You stay here," Paco said. "I will get some food."

"Thank you, Mr. Paco," Linda said.

Paco looked at the little girl, surprised that she had picked up on his name. He walked over to the bar and Moose, the American cantina owner, came toward him, wiping his hands on a towel.

"Who is that little girl?" Moose asked, nodding toward Linda. "What is she doing here?"

"Cantrell told me to bring her here. He has taken her *mamacita.*"

"And you have taken the little girl hostage?"

"I did not take her hostage," Paco said. "It was Cantrell and Michaels who took her."

"Maybe so, but you've got her now."

"*Si.* I have her now," Paco agreed. "We need some food."

Moose shook his head. "Hell no," he said. "You ain't gettin' no food for her. She can't stay here. She means trouble . . . big trouble."

Paco stroked his chin and nodded. "Yes," he said. "I, too, think she is trouble."

"Then get her out of here."

"Where can I take her?"

"I don't know. I don't care. Just get her the hell out of here!"

"I do not know where to take her. I think I will have to kill her."

Paco started back toward Linda's table.

"Wait a minute!" Moose called. Paco stopped.

"Are you serious? You could just kill her, like that?"

"*Si,*" Paco said easily.

"No," Moose said. "No, don't do that." He sighed. "I'll get Rosita to look after her."

"Rosita will do this?"

"Yeah," Moose said. "The problem is, she'll want to keep her."

● ● ●

Moose and his Mexican wife, Rosita, lived in an apartment upstairs over the cantina. The apartment was reached by an outside stairway so that it truly was separated from the cantina. Linda was upstairs in that apartment now, being put to bed in the spare bedroom.

The bedroom had not always been a spare room. At one time it had been the bedroom of Maria, Moose and Rosita's child. Maria had died two years earlier and Rosita had never recovered. Having a five-year-old girl suddenly entrusted to her care again, after all this time, was like a gift from heaven.

"Are you hungry, little one?" Rosita asked.

"No, thank you," Linda replied.

"Are you thirsty?"

"No, thank you."

"Is there anything Rosita can get for you?"

"I want my mother," Linda said.

Rosita put her arms around the little girl and held her close to her ample bosom. More than anything in the world, she would like to keep this child as her own, keep her to replace the one she had lost.

But she knew she could not. The *mamacita* of this child would cry for her as Rosita had cried for Maria. There was no one who could bring Maria back to Rosita. But Rosita could take this little one back to her *madre*.

"I will take you to her," Rosita said. "I promise you, I will take you to your *mamacita*." She lay Linda down. "Sleep now," she said. "Rosita will not let anything happen to you."

The Next Morning

"What the hell? Where is she? Where's the woman?" Cantrell shouted.

"What?" Michaels answered, sitting up and rubbing his eyes. "What's wrong?"

"What's wrong? I'll tell you what's wrong, you dumb bastard! You let the Adams woman get away!"

"I let the woman get away? What makes you think I did it?"

"You were the last one with her!" Cantrell screamed in anger. "Did you tie her up?"

"Yes," Michaels said, though even as he said it, he knew he was lying. He had been so tired, and so relaxed afterward, that he had fallen instantly to sleep.

"Well, you should've watched her."

"I was asleep, just like you was," Michaels said. "Anyway, what difference does it make?"

"It makes a lot of difference. She knows our names, she can identify us. You want to spend the rest of your life in Mexico, eatin' beans and tortillas? If she makes it back alive, we can't ever come back to the States."

"Hell, she probably won't even make it through the desert," Michaels said.

"She's stronger than you think," Cantrell said. "Didn't you notice her yesterday? She never complained once."

"So what are we going to do?"

"What are we goin' to do? We're goin' after her, you dumb shit," Cantrell raged.

"What are we goin' to do with her when we find her?"

"We're goin' to kill her," Cantrell said flatly. "Hell, she wasn't all that good a fuck anyway."

Boyd picked up Curly's trail at first light. He hadn't followed it too far before he noticed that the horse had broken stride, badly. Reading the sign told the story. In his desperate attempt to flee, Curly had ridden his horse into the ground. The four-hour lead Curly had meant nothing now. Boyd would catch up with him, of that he had no doubt.

Boyd found Curly's horse about mid-morning. The animal was still alive, though only barely. His nostrils were flecked with blood, evidence that Curly had run his horse until its heart burst.

"I'm sorry, fella," Boyd said to the horse. "The evil bastard didn't even have the decency to put you out of your misery." Boyd patted the horse gently on the neck, then he put his pistol to the horse's head and pulled the trigger. Mercifully, the horse died instantly.

Boyd took a drink of water, poured some into his hat for his horse, then began walking, following Curly's footprints across the hot desert sand.

The sign continued to tell the story, as clearly as if Boyd were reading it off the front page of the *Tombstone Epitaph*. Right after Curly's horse went down, Curly had been so frightened that he started running. He managed to run for about a mile. After he quit running, he walked for another couple of miles.

Then the desert began to exact its toll from him. Curly started throwing things away. Boyd found the pistol belt, though the holster was empty: Curly did keep his pistol. Next Boyd found Curly's spurs, then his shirt, and finally an empty canteen.

Within another mile Boyd found indications that Curly was beginning to have a difficult time staying on his feet. There were marks in the sand where Curly would fall, crawl for a few feet, then get up and lunge ahead for a few feet more before he would fall again.

Suddenly Boyd was startled to hear a train whistle ahead of him. He had been walking his horse but now he remounted. He hadn't realized that he was this close to a railroad track, and for the first time he began to worry about Curly actually getting away from him.

"Sorry, Horse," Boyd said. "But if Curly gets to that train before we do, I'm goin' to lose him."

Boyd urged his horse into a trot, even though he knew the horse was on the verge of dehydration and exhaustion. But he was caught upon the horns of a dilemma. He did not want his horse to wind up the way Curly's horse had wound up, but neither did he want Curly to escape.

Boyd resolved to do all in his power to prevent Curly from making good his escape. Curly had no right to still be perpetrating crimes against society. By all legal and moral rights Curly should already be dead. He had murdered at least six people. He had raped Mrs. Pemberton, and her young fifteen-year-old daughter, Sue. For those crimes a jury of his peers had found him guilty in a court of law. A legally empowered judge had sentenced Curly and his brother to death by hanging.

But the gallows had been cheated. Taking two more lives, including the life of the judge who had sentenced them, Curly and Frank had made their escape. Since that escape they had taken part in a bank robbery and taken as hostage a mother and her young daughter. Boyd had no idea where Millie was now, or what her condition was, or what part, if any, Curly and Frank had played in the actual crime. But Curly was a party to it . . . and he did stand condemned for his earlier crimes. And for having escaped his earlier sentencing, if for no other reason, Boyd did not intend to let Curly get away. He would bring him to justice, one way or the other.

The train whistle sounded much closer, and Boyd pushed his horse into a lope. Boyd could hear the train, but he still couldn't see it. That was because he was now going up a long, rather steeply rising slope. The slope was high enough in front of him that it obstructed Boyd's view of the other side.

The horse was really beginning to struggle now, for the slope was not only very steep, the sand was quite deep. Boyd could hear the horse gasping for breath.

"No!" Boyd said. "No, don't give up on me now!" He urged the horse into a gallop and, to his amazement, the horse responded.

The train whistled again, this time right in front of him.

Finally Boyd reached the top of the long slope, and, from here, he could see the track. The train was, at this very minute, passing by in front of him. It was a freight train consisting of an engine and about a dozen box cars.

Boyd got an unpleasant surprise. Instead of a down slope, which would have allowed him to catch Curly, there was a sharp drop-off. What had been a slope going to the top of the hill, became a cliff on the other side. It was so steep he could barely go down on foot, let alone ride his horse.

Boyd leapt out of the saddle and looked toward the track. He saw Curly then, for the first time. The outlaw, even though near collapse, had somehow called upon a hidden reserve of strength. He was running now, and he managed to catch the last car. He hung on the ladder for a moment or two, then he climbed to the top.

Boyd walked back to his horse. It was covered with a white foam of sweat.

"Good horse," Boyd said. "Pete told me you could run all day, and he was right. You gave me all you had. Now it's up to me."

Boyd patted the horse a couple of times, then he snaked his rifle out of the saddle sheath and walked, almost leisurely, back over to the edge of the cliff. He looked down toward the train. The train had started down a slight decline and it was beginning to pick up speed. Curly was now over four hundred yards away.

Boyd jacked a round into the chamber of his long gun, then he raised the rear site and slid the gate up to a range-marking of five hundred yards. Crossing his legs, and resting his left elbow just inside his left knee, he raised the rifle to his shoulder, then sighted down the long, octagonal barrel.

The distance opened to about five hundred yards. He was shooting down, his target was at an angle, it was moving at better than twenty miles per hour, and it was a little over a quarter of a mile away.

Boyd took in a deep breath, let half of the air out, then held it. Curly was still standing on top of the retreating box car, dancing a taunting little jig. From this distance Curly was not much bigger than the front site itself.

Slowly . . . ever so slowly . . . Boyd began squeezing the trigger.

Curly had seen Boyd take his rifle from his saddle holster, then sit down near the edge of the cliff.

The train was picking up speed, moving faster now than a good horse could gallop. The car was rattling and shaking and Curly was having a difficult time standing. He realized that he should get down, not only to help maintain his balance on the top of the rapidly moving train, but also to make himself a smaller target. But he felt compelled to make some gesture of defiance, some way to extract victory from the ordeal McMasters had put him through for the last twenty-four hours. Instead of sitting down, he hurled a challenge, knowing it couldn't be heard, but feeling some satisfaction from it, nevertheless.

"To hell with you!" he shouted, though he knew that distance and the sound of the train would prevent McMasters from hearing him. "You son of a bitch! You've run me ragged! You killed my brother! You made me run my horse to death! Well I beat you, Mister Captain McMasters! I beat you again!"

The gun boomed and Boyd felt the heavy recoil against his shoulder. A puff of smoke billowed out from the end of the gun, then drifted away.

"Shoot me off the train if you think you can!" Curly shouted. "You're nearly half a mile a way you . . ." in absolute silence Curly saw a puff of smoke from the end of the rifle, and he saw McMasters roll back with the recoil. ". . . stupid son of a . . ." Curly felt a blow to his chest, like being kicked by a mule. Involuntarily he spit out the last word. ". . . bitch!" He grabbed his stomach.

As the smoke cleared away, Boyd saw Curly grab his stomach, then tumble off the back of the train. Leaving his horse, Boyd scrambled down the steep side of the hill, then ran across the open plain between the cliff and the track, following the scar of Curly's footprints through the sand. It took him a couple of minutes to reach Curly's body. When he got there he saw that at least two chunks of the bullet had hit Curly in the heart. He was probably dead before he ever fell from the train. He went through Curly's clothes and, as he had with Frank, found five two-thousand-dollar packets.

"You dumb bastard," Boyd said under his breath. "You didn't even get the chance to buy a drink with the money."

Brushing his hands together, Boyd went back for his horse, then led it down to the track. He pulled out the spade and buried Curly, marking his grave the way he had Frank's. The only difference was the shell casing he used to hold the rolled-up piece of paper. For this one he used one of the .70-caliber shell casings.

Millie had ridden through most of the night, so exhausted that she was now nearly passed out in the saddle. She had lost all track of time and place. She wasn't even aware of when the sun came up. It seemed to her that one instant it was dark and the next it was light. It had gone from cold to hot, all within the blink of an eye.

She had enough presense of mind to realize that, as the sun was rising in front and to the left of her, she must be heading southeast. She didn't know if that was the direction she should be heading, she only knew that she was, with every step Dandy took, getting farther away from Cantrell and Michaels. And, for the moment, that was the most driving instinct she had.

Dandy stumbled once, and nearly went down, and Millie gasped in fear. Was her horse about to die?

"No," she said. "Oh, Dandy, poor Dandy, don't die on me," she said. She realized that if her horse did die she would be stranded in the desert, all alone, and with no means of escape.

"Water. If I could only get some water."

Ahead of her, she saw the shimmering waves of heat which made it look as if there were a lake there. She knew about mirages, and she knew better than to be caught up by one.

Dandy must be thirsty, too, she thought. He has been going all night, without stop. And he had gone all day yesterday, as well. She had at least been able to ride.

Ride! That's it, she thought. She shouldn't ride anymore. If she were going to spare her horse, she should at least get off and walk.

"No, I can't get off and walk," she said, arguing aloud with herself. "If I walk they'll catch me!"

Then she realized that even yesterday, they had walked their horses. If Dandy is tired, so their horses must be as well. If they don't rest their horses, they'll kill them.

Millie slid down from the saddle, wincing in pain, not only from two days of saddle sores, but also from the effect of the brutal rape she had experienced last night. She held onto the stirrup, then started walking with the horse.

"Find us some water, Dandy," she said to to her horse. "It's up to you now. If you want a drink, find us some water."

Dandy stumbled on through the desert with Millie hanging on. She had long periods of time when she felt almost as if she had lost consciousness. And yet, she knew that couldn't be, because she continued to walk.

"Wait, Dandy," she finally said. "Stop. I've got to rest, just a bit. Just a bit," she said.

Dandy stopped and Millie sat down.

Thirteen

Boyd crossed the west branch of the Santa Cruz River at noon. There he was able to refill his canteen and water his horse so that when he continued rider and horse were refreshed. It was about mid-afternoon when Boyd saw a horse, standing alone in the middle of the desert. He thought it was standing alone until he got a little closer, then he saw something bright yellow on the ground.

Because of the yellow, he knew immediately that it had to be Mrs. Adams, and he urged his horse into a short but rapid gallop, closing the gap between them. Taking his canteen, he leaped down from the horse and hurried over to her, saying a short but sincere prayer that she still be alive. As soon as he reached her, he knew that she was.

"Mrs. Adams! Mrs. Adams!" he said.

Millie opened her eyes.

"Captain McMasters," she said. "I'm saved."

Boyd was sitting in the shade of a large saguaro, smoking one of his few remaining cigarillos, watching the sun die with a blaze of color. The Cababi Mountains made a long, jagged ridge to the west, while to the north he could see the Sierritas, and, purple with distance in the east, the Dragoons. The terrible heat of the day was abating now, and the desert was quiet and the air was still and pleasant. Behind him, the west branch of the Santa Cruz bubbled pleasantly.

Close by, Millie was sleeping on a blanket he had put out for her. During the heat of the afternoon he had spread a tarp across a couple of mesquite branches to shade her from the sun. Refreshed by drink and by getting into the river so that her clothes were wet, the slow evaporation had kept her cool for the entire afternoon, thus allowing her to rest.

She had ridden, nonstop, from the time she escaped Cantrell and Michaels. She was almost delirious by the time Boyd found her, and if he had been one more day in finding her, she wouldn't have made it.

Earlier in the afternoon Boyd had killed a rattlesnake. Now the snake was cooking over a small fire. It and beans with a couple of peppers would make tonight's supper.

Boyd ached to get after Cantrell and Michaels, and the little girl, but it was more important now that he see to Millie Adams. He had already worked out a plan. They would spend the night here on the river, then before dawn tomorrow she would be rested and revived enough for him to take her back to the railroad. There they would wait for the next passenger train going north. She could take it up to Calabasas, and there take a train back to Crittenden. With her safely out of the way, Boyd could concentrate on finding the little girl and bringing the other three men in. The third man, he had learned, was a Mexican named Paco. Paco was the one who had taken Linda.

The sun set and the night sky displayed its jewelry in the diamondlike scatter of stars. The moon was a brilliant silver orb, bright enough so that the Dragoon Mountains were still visible. Within the campsite itself, the small fire made a tiny bubble of wavering orange light.

"Uhhmmm. What is that heavenly smell?" Millie asked.

She had been absolutely silent for so long that Boyd, who was used to being alone with his own thoughts, had forgotten about her and was startled by her words. He recovered quickly.

"Hello," he said. "How are you feeling?"

Millie sat up and ran her hand through her hair. "Much better than I look, I'm certain," she said.

Boyd smiled. "You're as pretty now as you were the first time I saw you."

"Oh, my, that doesn't say much for the way I looked then," Millie said.

"I mean, uh . . ." Boyd stammered, and Millie laughed.

"I was teasing you," she said. "I know what you meant and I thank you for it. But you didn't answer my question. What is that delightful aroma?"

"It's our supper," Boyd said. He didn't specifically tell her it was rattlesnake, for fear she would be put off by it.

"It smells like you're cooking meat. You must have found some game."

"Yes, I did," Boyd said. Boyd saw the bruises on her wrists, and he nodded toward them. "There's some aloe plant over there,'' he said. "If you rub the juice from the leaves on a wound, it stops the pain. Would you like me to rub some on your wrists?''

Millie looked down at them, then held them out in front of her. "Yes, please,'' she said.

Boyd cut several leaves, then came back and began breaking them, rubbing the juice into the bruises on her wrists.

"How does that feel?'' he asked.

"Much better, thank you,'' she replied. She sighed. "It's too bad there isn't something you can rub onto my soul.''

"Bad?''

"Beyond bad,'' she said. She blinked a couple of times and tears began sliding down her face. Boyd went over to his saddlebag and pulled out a bottle.

"Maybe this will help,'' he said, handing it to her. "It helped me a little after . . .'' He paused, then went on, thinking that perhaps mentioning it would make it a bit easier for Millie. "After my wife was raped and murdered,'' he said.

Millie accepted the bottle, then took a big swallow of whiskey. She handed the bottle back.

"In a way she was the lucky one,'' she said.

Boyd looked at her strangely.

"I'm sorry,'' Millie said quickly. "I know you don't feel that way. But, after what happened to me out there, I'll never be the same. For the rest of my life people will look at me differently. Some will even blame me.''

"Who could blame you?'' Boyd asked.

"You'd be surprised,'' Millie replied. She forced a smile, as if attempting to put an unpleasant subject behind her. "Tell me, Captain McMasters, are we just going to smell the supper? Or do we actually get to eat it?''

Boyd laughed. ''We actually get to eat it,'' he said. ''I think it's about ready.''

Boyd served Millie from the tin plate he had. She also got the knife and fork. He ate directly from the skillet, using a spoon and his jackknife. They ate in silence for a few moments; Boyd, because it was his way, and Millie, because she was too busy enjoying her food to talk. Finally, with a sigh of satisfaction, she set the plate down.

''Have you ever been to France, Captain Mc-Masters?''

''I'm afraid not,'' Boyd answered.

''My father took me to Paris when I was eighteen,'' Millie said. ''There is a cafe just off the Champs-Elysees where you can get *coq-au-vin* and truly wonderful *baguettes* of bread. When we ate there I thought I had gone to heaven, for I had never tasted anything as wonderful in my life. And never since''—she paused and looked over at him, her eyes shining brightly in the dying light of the fire—''until now,'' she concluded.

Boyd chuckled. ''If you knew what it was, I'm not sure you would say that.''

''It was rattlesnake,'' Millie said.

Boyd looked surprised. ''Yes, it was,'' he said.

''I woke up once during the afternoon and saw you skinning it,'' she said. She put her hand on his. ''And I still say this is the most wonderful meal I have ever eaten.''

''I'm glad you think so,'' Boyd said. ''And I'll be selfish enough to take the credit for it, even though the Indians say that hunger is the best seasoning.'' Boyd took her pan and his skillet, then started to walk away.

"Where . . . where are you going?" Millie asked in a frightened voice.

"Just down beside the river to clean the dishes," Boyd said. "It's not more than twenty yards away. I'll be right back."

"I'm sorry," Millie said. "I'm being a baby, I know. I'm still a little frightened."

"You have every right to be frightened," Boyd said. He smiled. "And don't worry, even if you can't see me, I'll still be able to see you by the light of the fire. You just take it easy, I'll be right back."

Boyd was asleep when she called out to him in the middle of the night.

"Captain McMasters? Captain McMasters?" she called in a quiet voice.

"Yes."

"I'm cold. May I lie next to you?"

"If you want to. Come on over." Boyd heard the rustling noise of her moving, then he felt the blanket being thrown down beside him. She lay down beside him and shivered.

"Please," Millie said. "Please hold me."

Boyd put his arms around her and pulled her to him to comfort her. He could feel her heartbeat.

"Hold me tighter," Millie said.

Boyd pulled her closer to him and he could feel her thighs pressed against him, her breasts against his chest. He could also feel his excitement rise and, almost unintentionally it seemed, he felt her rub her sex against him. "I need to know," she said.

"I beg your pardon?"

"I need to know," she said again.

Boyd was confused. "Need to know what?"

"Those men," Millie said. "The things they did to me." She shivered again, and Boyd knew that this time it wasn't from the cold. "It was awful with them. And it wasn't good with my husband. Before ..." She paused. "Do you remember you asked why I had married Richard?"

"I had no business prying," Boyd replied.

"It is a legitimate question," Millie said. "I married Richard to escape an uncomfortable situation. You see I had a fiance whom I loved dearly. We ... we had sex, and it was wonderful. But he was killed, and I was left to face a scandal alone, so my father arranged for me to marry Richard."

"I see," Boyd said.

"I need to know," Millie said again. "I need to know if I will ever again be able to find pleasure with a man. I need to know if a man will ever again find me desirable."

"Of course you will. And what man couldn't find you desirable?"

"Do you?"

"Yes, I find you very desirable."

Millie rubbed against him again and he felt himself growing hard.

"Would you make love to me?" she asked.

"Mrs. Adams ..."

"Please, call me Millie."

"Millie, you are very defenseless right now. It would be unfair ... unchivalrous of me to take advantage of this situation."

"I want you to take advantage," Millie said. "Please,

Boyd. I can call you Boyd?''

"Yes, if you want.''

"Boyd, if I don't do this now, tonight, with you, with someone I trust, then I may never do it again. And if I never do it again, that means I am sentenced to live the rest of my life without love. Please, those awful men took so much from me. Don't let them take that as well. Make love to me, Boyd.''

By now her face was just a breath away from Boyd's face, and he put his hand on her cheek and pulled her to him so he could kiss her. He was surprised by the urgency of her response, the eagerness of her tongue. He put aside the thought that had bothered him earlier. She wasn't a defenseless victim, she was a woman, a desirable woman, who wanted him as badly as he wanted her. He turned his body toward her so that he could rub against her.

"Wait,'' she said, quietly. "Let me get undressed.''

Millie began unfastening the buttons that held her riding garment closed. That which had defeated her when she was with Cantrell and Michaels, now worked in her favor, for it required only a few seconds to open the dress all the way, then slip out of it so that she was totally naked on the blanket.

Quickly, Boyd removed his own clothes, looking at the woman who lay illuminated by the bright light of the moon. She was breathtakingly beautiful. Her skin was nearly translucent, her breasts small but well formed and uplifted. Her hips flared out with just the right amount of curve, and the crowning bush was full and luxurious.

Within a moment Boyd was as naked as she.

"Oh,'' Millie said. "You are a good-looking man.''

She ran her hand down his flat stomach, then felt his organ. "Yes," she said, as she wrapped her hand around it. "I had almost forgotten how wonderful it can feel to hold onto something like this."

Boyd put his hand on her inner thigh then moved it up. He felt her stiffen and he stopped.

"What is it?" Boyd asked.

"Nothing," Millie said. For a moment she recalled, too vividly, the coarse, rough hands of Cantrell when he had forced her thighs open.

Then Boyd saw the bruises on the insides of her thighs, and he pulled his hand away.

"No, please, don't stop!" Millie said, grabbing his hand and pulling it back down, not only on her thighs, but on the lips of her sex. "I have to do this, don't you understand? I must be a woman again!"

Gently, Boyd moved his fingers through the lips of her sex, emboldened when he felt her grow slick with desire. She moaned with pleasure and began moving her own hand up and down his shaft, feeling its throbbing heat. For fully a minute Boyd's fingers teased, probed, stroked, and massaged until Millie was squirming in uncontrollable desire.

"I'm ready for you," Millie finally said. "I want it. I want you in me now, please."

Boyd moved over her and she guided him into the accommodating damp folds of flesh. She was well lubricated with the copious flowing of her sex, and when Millie put her hands around behind Boyd and pulled forward, he slipped in easily. She moaned and thrust up against him, pulling him deep inside her.

As Millie writhed in ecstasy beneath him, Boyd put his mouth to her neck. He could feel her neck muscles twitching, and he opened his mouth to suck on the creamy white flesh. He moved from her neck down to her breast and began sucking one of the nipples, flipping it with his tongue. He could hear her gasps and moans of pleasure as he continued to thrust against her.

Boyd heard Millie's gasps and moans rise in intensity, and he could tell by the increase of her movements and the spasmodic action of her hips that she was nearing orgasm. He rode with her, and when she peaked, her contractions sucked the juices from deep within Boyd's body. It was a total, all-consuming orgasm, and for an instant he felt keenly with every inch of his body that was in contact with Millie's naked skin.

Boyd lay on top of Millie for a few seconds, then he rolled to one side. He put his arm out and Millie cuddled against it. His hand was positioned just over her breast and Millie reached up and brought it down so he was holding it. They were quiet for a moment, then Millie spoke.

"Thank you," she said, feelingly. "Now I know that, with the right man, it can be beautiful and wonderful. I am a woman again."

Pajaraito

"Rosita," Moose said, coming into the kitchen of the cantina to speak to his wife. "Rosita, where is the little girl?"

"Linda is sleeping. That is where all little girls her age should be at this time of night," Rosita replied.

"Linda? Why are you callin' her Linda?"

"Because that's her name."

"Yeah? Well, as far as you are concerned, she ain't got no name."

"Why do you say she has no name?"

Moose waved his hand as if dismissing the little girl and the question.

"Because she don't even exist as far as we're concerned. The less we have to do with her, the better off we are." He saw two pieces of paper tacked to the wall. One piece of paper had a crude drawing of a tree. The other had a horse. "What is that?" he asked, pointing to the drawings.

Rosita smiled broadly. "They are pictures Linda drew for me today. They are very good, are they not?"

"Get rid of them!" Moose said. He jerked them off the wall, and wadded them up.

"Give them back to me!" Rosita screamed, reaching for them.

"Get away!" Moose said gruffly. He slapped Rosita hard, then he tossed the two wadded-up drawings into the flames of the kitchen range.

"Why did you do that?" Rosita asked, holding her hand over the swelling under her eye. "She made the pictures for me."

"That's why I did it," Moose growled. "Now, go up there and get the kid ready. I want you to give her to Paco."

"Why do you say give her to Paco? You say to me that Paco does not want her. You say to me I am to keep her."

"You were just supposed to keep her out of sight, that's all," Moose said. "You weren't gettin' her to raise. She belongs to Paco."

"She does not belong to Paco. She belongs to her *mamacita*."

Moose chortled. "You ain't thinkin' you're the brat's *mamacita*, are you?"

"No," Rosita said. "I am talking about her real *mamacita*."

"Her real *mamacita?* Woman, what's gotten into you? I told you, we can't get involved in this. Now give her to Paco like I told you to."

"What will Paco do with her?"

"Who gives a shit what he does with her? As long as he gets her out of here, that's all that matters."

"What will he do with Linda?" Rosita asked again.

"Linda. Will you, for chrissake, quit callin' her Linda, like she's your long-lost sister or somethin'? What do you think he'll do with her? He is going to take her to Mexico and sell her. She's a pretty little blond-haired, blue-eyed girl. He'll find some nice family for her down there."

Rosita shook her head. "Such girls are not sold to families to be daughters. They are sold to be *putas.* Whores."

"Yeah, well, she'll probably make a fine whore in a couple of years. Anyway, what's so bad about being a whore? You were a whore when I met you. Hell, you still whore some when times is bad for us. Now you go up there and get her ready and give her to Paco like I said."

"Moose, *por favor,* let me keep her," Rosita begged.

"No, goddamnit!" Moose said. He drew back his hand as if he were going to hit her again, only this time Rosita jumped out of his way and grabbed a butcher knife.

"I will not let you hit me again!" she screamed at him, holding the knife in front of her.

Moose laughed, then relaxed his arm. "There," he said. "That's the spirit I like to see. Rosita the fighter, not Rosita the cow, moaning for her calf." He grew more gentle. "Rosita, maybe some day there will be another child for you. But this little girl isn't it. She is trouble, can't you see that? She is nothing but trouble. Now, be a good girl, and go get her ready for Paco."

Rosita held the knife for a moment longer, then, with a sigh, she put the knife on the table.

"*Sí,*" she said. "I will get her ready for Paco."

"That's my girl," Moose said. He got a strange, lustful look in his eyes. "And if you're particular nice to Paco, maybe you can get into some of his money, if you know what I mean."

"You want me to be a whore with Paco?"

"Yeah, well, just one more time, to tell him goodbye. He's a wealthy man right now. And he always did like you more'n any other whore in Pajarito. And why not? Aren't you the best lookin'?" he added.

"But you are my husband, Moose. You want me to do this?"

"Sure, why not? You can pick up some money, and then, later tonight, when we go to bed, you can tell me all about it."

"*Sí,*" Rosita said. "Tonight, I will tell you all about it."

Rosita left the kitchen and walked out into the cantina. It wasn't hard to find Paco. As Moose said, he was now the wealthiest man in Pajarito and every whore in the cantina was vying for his charms. Rosita heard that Paco had accommodated as many as he could last night and this morning. He hadn't yet visited any of the cribs to-night, obviously enjoying being pursued.

There was one whore sitting on his lap. The top of her dress was pulled down so that her breasts were showing, and she was running her fingers through Paco's hair. Another whore was sitting next to him with her hand inside his leg. A third had her legs up on his, with her skirt pulled all the way up to show that she was wearing nothing under the dress.

"Paco," Rosita said.

Paco looked up.

"Moose said you want to take the little girl with you."

"*Sí*," Paco replied. "I think I can sell her for much money in Mexico."

"When you are ready to leave, come to my room and I will give her to you," Rosita said.

"I will leave in the morning," Paco said. He smiled. "But maybe I can come to your room tonight?"

Rosita smiled back at him. "Are you a *toro* that you must have many cows?" she asked. "I think you are too tired for Rosita." She consciously turned her body to thrust out her hips.

Paco pushed the whore off his lap.

"Paco, no," the whore said. "You do not want her. She is married."

Paco grinned broadly. "It is more fun if she is married," he said. "How much do you want for me to go to your room?" he asked.

"I am told you have already been with three women," Rosita said. "Maybe you cannot be with another."

"I can be with another. How much do you want?"

"I want what you paid all three of the others to-gether."

Paco put his hand in his pocket and pulled out a twenty dollar bill. "This is more than I paid all three," he said. "But you had better be worth it."

"I am worth it," Rosita said. "Come with me." To the vocal disappointment of the other whores, she led him away with an exaggerated sway of her hips.

They walked through the beaded door, then up the outside set of stairs to the apartment over the cantina. When they stepped inside, Rosita put her finger to her lips.

"Shhh," she said. "I will check on the little one. I do not want her to wake while we are busy."

"She should watch," Paco said. "She should watch and learn, for this is to be her trade."

"There is time for that later," Rosita said. She pointed to her bedroom. "Go in there and wait for me."

"That is the bed where your husband fucks you?" Paco asked.

"Yes."

Paco grinned broadly. "Good, good. I want to fuck you in the bed where your husband fucks you."

Rosita stepped quietly into the other bedroom and saw Linda sleeping. Then she came back. She lit a candle, then began stripping out of her clothes, calling upon all the tricks of her professional experience to entice this man who would be her lover. She used a shadow here, a soft light there, a movement to hold her body just so. As if by magic the person who, just a few moments before had held a butcher knife out to her husband, now became a sensual creature.

"Now, this is what you want, isn't it?" she asked in

a husky, sexy voice, beckoning him to her nakedness.

"Yes, *senora*, this is what I want," Paco replied, obviously enjoying the use of the term denoting the fact that Rosita was married. He unbuckled his belt and slipped his pants down, but he didn't take them off.

"Come to me," Rosita said, lying back on the bed, spreading her legs for him. "You are so big, so *macho*, I know you can make me feel better than my husband." She put her hands on his naked thighs. One hand grasped his throbbing, hot shaft and moved it up into position. The other hand moved down his leg to the belt of his trousers, then to his knife. Her fingers wrapped around it.

Paco felt her moving him into position. He felt the head of his organ pushing against the lips of her sex. He felt something sharp, like a pin prick, at his belly.

"Now, my big, strong man," Rosita said. "Shove it in!"

Paco thrust forward hard, filling her with his manhood. He gasped, then opened his eyes and looked down into her face.

"*Que pasa?*" he asked in confusion. He pulled himself out, then raised up on his knees and looked down at his belly. He saw his knife, buried hilt-deep in his gut. He pulled it out, and as he did so, he filled his hands with his own blood. His eyes began to cloud over, then he fell forward. Rosita managed, at the last minute, to roll out from under him. She lay quietly beside him for a moment longer, then she reached over to put her hand over his heart.

He was dead.

Fourteen

The handle of the coffeepot Boyd had suspended over the open flames was so hot that he had to use his hat in order to pour a cup of coffee for Millie. It was before dawn and, after a breakfast of coffee and jerky, they were going to start back toward the track where Boyd would flag down a train for her.

He had just hung the pot up again when he sensed, rather than saw or heard, that someone was watching them. He had not saddled the horses yet, and he looked over at his saddle where his gunbelt and rifle lay. He put his hand down in his pocket and started to ease toward his guns, but whoever was watching him figured out what he was doing.

"Just stay right there, McMasters," a voice called. "Get your hand out of your pocket and there better not be a gun in it."

"Oh!" Millie gasped, and Boyd knew by the fear in that one word, that Millie had recognized that voice in the dark.

"Hello, Cantrell," Boyd said easily. "Why don't you and Michaels come on into the camp?" He held up his hands. "As you can see, I don't have a gun."

"Good, good, that's just the way I like it," Cantrell answered.

Boyd heard the sound of footsteps. A moment later two men materialized out of the darkness. They stood just in the outer bubble of light. Both were holding pistols leveled at him. Both had a haggard look about them.

"Well, now, ain't this cozy?" Cantrell said. "I'll just bet you two had a good ol' time here last night."

"I'm surprised to see you here," Boyd said. "I figured you would be in Mexico by now."

"Yeah, well, I've got a little unfinished business before I go off to Mexico," Cantrell said.

"Good," Boyd said.

Cantrell looked at him in surprise. "Good? What do you mean, good?"

"I mean you've done my work for me," Boyd answered easily. "Now I don't have to come down there to look for you. I've already found you."

Cantrell laughed. "You've already found us? Mister, are you crazy or what? You ain't found us, we've found you."

"If you want to look at it that way," Boyd said.

"Where's the Dobbs boys?" Michaels asked.

"I killed them," Boyd answered. "Both of them."

Cantrell nodded. "Yeah, I figured as much," he said. He smiled. "Well, now, ain't that a break for us? Iffen you killed 'em, you got their share of the money on you. We'll just take that back."

"Oh, I didn't bother with the money," Boyd said easily.

"You didn't bother with the money? What the hell do you mean you didn't bother with the money?"

"Why should I?"

"Mister, you ain't makin' a hell of a lot of sense, you know that?"

"Oh, I think I am making sense," Boyd said. "I was in the middle of the desert, trying to travel light, trying to hunt you boys down. I've got to hand it to you, you did give me a run for it before I caught up with you. Anyway, I didn't see any sense in being burdened down by a bunch of counterfeit money so I . . ."

"Counterfeit money?" Cantrell shouted. "What the hell you talkin' about, counterfeit money?"

"Well, you didn't think Mr. Adams was going to bring back real money to you, did you?"

"He did bring back real money," Michaels said.

Boyd chuckled. "No, I'm afraid not. You see, one of the things the Cattleman's Protective Association does when they take on a bank to protect is, we give them a big bundle of counterfeit money to use just in case something like this happens. You've gone to all this trouble for nothing."

"What are we goin' to do, Cantrell?" Michaels asked.

"Nothin'," Michaels replied. He saw Boyd stepping toward the fire. "What are you doin'?" he growled, raising his gun.

"I was just going to offer you men some coffee," Boyd said easily. "You look pretty haggard. I imagine you've had a rough time with it."

"Get away from the fire." Cantrell said, making a motion with his pistol.

Boyd moved over toward Millie and put his arms around her.

"Mister, you ain't foolin' nobody with that counterfeit money business," he said. "I figure you've got that twenty thousand on you and . . ."

Suddenly there was a series of loud explosions coming from the fire. Boyd was ready for it, and when it started popping he was holding Millie. He dived behind his saddle, taking her with him. As he went over the saddle he grabbed his pistol, then, while still lying on the ground, he spun back around with his pistol in his hand, the hammer already coming back.

Both Michaels and Cantrell were screaming and jumping around, trying to dodge whatever was after them.

"You son of a bitch!" Cantrell shouted, firing into the darkness in Boyd's general direction. Boyd heard the bullet whiz by overhead, and he answered fire, placing his bullet in Cantrell's heart. A second shot, this one in the forehead, brought down Michaels, who was also firing.

After the last explosion detonated, Boyd jumped up from his position behind the saddle, then walked over to look down at the two outlaws.

"Are they . . . dead?" Millie asked.

"Yes, both of them," Boyd said, lowering his pistol. "They won't be giving anyone else any trouble."

"Oh, thank God," Millie said.

Boyd came back to his saddle and slipped his pistol into the holster.

"What happened? What was all that?"

"When I took my hand out of my pockets, I palmed five cartridges," Boyd explained. "When I went over for coffee, I dropped them into the fire. Then I just waited for them to go off."

It was full light by the time Boyd had both outlaws buried. Millie was sitting over by the two saddles, wait-

ing patiently as Boyd worked. Unlike the other two outlaws, Cantrell and Michaels were carrying their money
in the original bag that Adams had put it in.

"Boyd, the money," Millie said.

"What about it?"

"Were you telling the outlaws the truth? Is it really
counterfeit?"

Boyd smiled and shook his head. "It's not counterfeit
at all," he said. "It's as good as gold. I was just looking
for some way to keep them talking. I figured as long as
they were talking, they weren't shooting and . . ."

"Linda!" Millie suddenly shouted with a cry of joy.
She jumped up from the saddle and started running. Surprised, Boyd turned around and saw a single horse coming toward them. The horse was being ridden by a
woman and she was carrying a child in front of her.

"Mother!" Linda called back.

The woman on the horse stopped, then set Linda
down. Linda and Millie ran toward each other, meeting
halfway in a big embrace. Boyd walked out to see the
woman.

"You are the one they call McMasters?" the woman
asked.

"Yes."

"I am Rosita Jones."

"Jones?"

"I am married to a gringo," Rosita said. She untied
a small, cloth bag from her saddle and handed it down
to Boyd. Boyd opened it and looked inside. It was filled
with money. "That is the money Paco had," she said.

"Where is Paco now?" Boyd asked.

"Paco is dead. I killed him."

"How do I know this is true?"

Rosita pointed to the bag. "Would you have the money if this were not true?" she asked.

Boyd smiled. "I guess not."

"How much money was in the bag?" Rosita asked.

"You did not count it?"

Rosita shook her head. "I did not want to count it, *señor*," she said. "Maybe if I counted it, I would not want to give it back. I would take it all instead of the little amount I did take."

"How much did you take?"

"I took one thousand dollars, *señor*. I know this is the reward for Paco, for he himself told me."

Boyd held up the sack. "This isn't how the rewards are paid."

"That is how the reward is paid to me, *señor*," Rosita said. "I cannot go back to Pajarito. I must go now to Mexico. I cannot wait for the way the reward is paid. I will do it this way, and I think you will make it right for me."

Boyd stroked his cheek as he studied her. "All right." He finally nodded. "I'll make it right for you."

"The little girl is with her *mamacita* now?"

"Yes."

"That is good," Rosita said. "That is very good." She turned and started riding south.

Boyd heard a distant roll of thunder. Looking to the west, he saw a dark bank of clouds building up. The rain wouldn't get here, he knew. The Cababi Mountains would steal what moisture the clouds had. But it might make the ride back to Crittenden a bit cooler. Looking back at the happy expressions on the faces of Millie and Linda, he knew the ride would be more pleasant.

Watch for

BIG .70

4th in the sizzling McMASTERS series
from Jove

Coming in December!

If you enjoyed this book, subscribe now and get...

TWO FREE

A $7.00 VALUE—

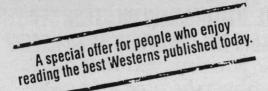

A special offer for people who enjoy reading the best Westerns published today.

WESTERNS!

NO OBLIGATION

Mail the coupon below

To start your subscription and receive 2 FREE WESTERNS, fill out the coupon below and mail it today. We'll send your first shipment which includes 2 FREE BOOKS as soon as we receive it.

Mail To: **True Value Home Subscription Services, Inc.** P.O. Box 5235
120 Brighton Road, Clifton, New Jersey 07015-5235

YES! I want to start reviewing the very best Westerns being published today. Send me my first shipment of 6 Westerns for me to preview FREE for 10 days. If I decide to keep them, I'll pay for just 4 of the books at the low subscriber price of $2.75 each; a total $11.00 (a $21.00 value). Then each month I'll receive the 6 newest and best Westerns to preview Free for 10 days. If I'm not satisfied I may return them within 10 days and owe nothing. Otherwise I'll be billed at the special low subscriber rate of $2.75 each; a total of $16.50 (at least a $21.00 value) and save $4.50 off the publishers price. There are never any shipping, handling or other hidden charges. I understand I am under no obligation to purchase any number of books and I can cancel my subscription at any time, no questions asked. In any case the 2 FREE books are mine to keep.

Name _____

Street Address _____ Apt. No. _____

City _____ State _____ Zip Code _____

Telephone _____

Signature _____
(if under 18 parent or guardian must sign)

Terms and prices subject to change. Orders subject
to acceptance by True Value Home Subscription
Services, Inc.

11731-5